Children
of the
Dark

ALSO BY STEVE HAYES

Gun for Revenge

Packing Iron

A Coffin for Santa Rosa

Trail of the Hanged Man

Viva Gringo!

A Woman to Die For

The Osprey Dilemma

Feral

Dead End

Tomorrow, Utopia

Killer Smile

Fanatics

Googies: Coffee Shop to the Stars, Vols 1 and 2

Sherlock Holmes and the Queen of Diamonds

Children
of the
Dark

by Steve Hayes

BearManor Fiction
2011

Children of the Dark

For information, address:

BearManor Fiction
P. O. Box 71426
Albany, GA 31708

bearmanorfiction.com

Cover design by John Teehan

Typesetting and layout by John Teehan

Published in the USA by BearManor Fiction

ISBN—1-59393-372-X
978-1-59393-372-2

For David Whitehead

Table of Contents

December Déjà Vu 1

The Gun 9

Spare the Children.. 13

Of Kites, Tide Pools and Fireflies 27

St. Christopher and the Little Fisherman....................... 37

The Butterfly Bomb 45

Jeunesse.. 51

Humpty Dumpty Had a Great Fall................................. 59

Three Caballeros.. 65

The Sins of the Father 69

December Déjà Vu

Study the past if you would divine the future
                                                        – Confucius

Rosario Chavez was dreaming about winning the California lottery when the earthquake hit at four-thirty-three that December 21st morning. It was a powerful quake, registering 6.8 on the Richter Scale, and its epicenter was four miles northeast of the city of San Fernando. The violent shaking threw Rosario, his wife, Theresa, and their three children out of their beds, broke all the windows and cracked the ceiling. Three massive aftershocks followed almost immediately. Gas and water mains broke, fires started, walls caved in, and by the time the earth had completely stopped shaking, the whole apartment complex had collapsed.

The old rundown two-story stucco building stood on land that had once belonged to the historic San Fernando Mission; now, two hundred years later, it was just one of many decrepit buildings occupied by impoverished Mexican families, many of whom were living six and eight to a room. The lucky ones, who lived on the second floor, were able to crawl out of the rubble unaided. The families on the ground floor weren't so lucky; it took firemen and rescue workers hours of digging before they eventually found them and dragged them out. Incredibly, no one was killed. But many were injured and suffering from shock.

Rosario's left wrist was broken, Theresa had a deep cut on her forehead, and two of their children, Carlos and Julio, were covered in cuts and bruises. No one knew how their third child, ten-year-old Celia, was—she was still buried under a mountain of rubble.

It was dark where Celia Chavez lay trapped among the debris. She was still dazed by a blow she'd received from a falling beam, and though she could vaguely hear the shouts and noise of the rescue workers as they dug out the other survivors, she had no idea how close they were or if they were digging in her direction. Nor did she know exactly where she was. She remembered being thrown out of her bed with her two younger brothers, remembered feeling the floor shaking under her, remembered everyone screaming and then, just as suddenly as it began, the earthquake stopped; there was a brief stillness, a frightening silence quickly followed by three more jolting shocks that brought the ceiling down on top of her. Stunned, she felt the floor give way; then she was falling, her screams hidden by the loud rending, splintering noise of the building collapsing all around her. She landed hard, the breath knocked out of her. She tried to move, but something heavy fell on her head and everything went black.

When she'd first regained consciousness and realized she was buried alive, she'd been too traumatized to scream. But as time dragged by, shock melted into terror and she was able to scream for help. She screamed until she was hoarse; then, when no one answered her, she gave up and began to cry. She cried until she was too tired to cry anymore. Still no one came or called out to her. Demoralized and thirsty, she fought down her panic and concentrated all her remaining strength on trying to dig her way out. It was useless: huge slabs of concrete, splintered beams and broken chunks of flooring formed a cage around her. She tried to push things aside, but everything was too heavy for her to move and wedged too close together for her to crawl through. The smell of gas, leaking from a ruptured main, permeated the air she was breathing. She began to pray, begging God to save her. She prayed for several minutes, punctuating her prayers with Hail Marys in the hope that if God were too busy to help, perhaps the Blessed Virgin might be listening. But no help came and Celia was forced to realize that she was alone, trapped in a space barely large enough to turn around in, unable to tell anyone where she was.

Fearful and exhausted, she closed her eyes and listened to the muffled sounds of the rescue workers digging high above her. Time dragged by. Celia had no idea how much time, because every second seemed like an hour; every hour an eternity. The smell of leaking gas grew stronger. Gradually, she became groggy. She felt herself growing sleepy. She didn't remember dozing off, but she must have because the next thing she heard was the noise of someone crawling toward her. Elated, she opened her eyes. By now, she was accustomed to the darkness and could see everything about her. But she was not prepared for the sight facing her just beyond her feet: a strange little Indian girl of about four or five sat watching her.

The little girl smelled of smoke. Her dark hair was burned off close to her scalp, her round brown face smudged with dirt, and her handmade beaded doeskin dress badly singed in places as if she'd been in a fire.

Celia, who knew all the other children in the apartment building, grog-gily rubbed her eyes to make sure she wasn't seeing things. Then, as the little girl continued to sit there watching her, Celia realized she must be real and asked her in Spanish who she was.

The little girl smiled, her black eyes bright and friendly as she looked fixedly at Celia, but said nothing. Celia next asked her where she'd come from and how she'd gotten into the tiny cramped space. Again, the little girl smiled but didn't speak. Celia, deciding the child might not understand Spanish, repeated all her questions in English. Still the little girl didn't say anything.

"Can't you talk?" Celia asked her.

The little girl tilted her head, first to the left, then to the right, as if try-ing to understand what Celia was saying. She then got to her knees, turned around so she was facing away from Celia, looked back and crooked one finger at her.

"You want me to follow you?" Celia said.

The little girl beckoned with her finger again. Celia squirmed around in the cramped space until she was on her hands and knees and then crawled close to the little girl.

"Now what?"

The little girl squeezed through a very small opening in the tangled web of debris ahead of her, turned and waited for Celia to follow.

"I can't get through there," Celia said. "I'm too big."

The little girl reached back through the opening with one hand and motioned for Celia to grab hold of it. Celia hesitated. She didn't know why but she felt uneasy about touching the quiet, mysterious child. The little girl motioned again. Reluctantly, Celia grasped her hand. It felt cold and clam-my. Celia shivered and tried to let go, but the little girl wouldn't let her. She tugged, pulling Celia close to the opening. Celia's shoulder pressed against a piece of flooring that she'd previously tried to move, but couldn't. Now, amaz-ingly, it moved aside, allowing her enough room to squeeze through.

Once Celia was safely beside her, the little girl let go of her hand and beck-oned for Celia to follow her. Celia obeyed. Together they wriggled, crawled, and squeezed through a maze of openings in the seemingly impenetrable mountain of rubble piled all around them. It was slow, exhausting work. They could only move forward a few inches at a time. Hours passed. Celia no longer smelled gas leaking. Her head cleared. But dust filled her eyes and clogged her throat and jagged edges cut her hands and splinters buried into her bare flesh. She had no idea in which direction she was going; sometimes it felt as though they were climbing upward, other times, downward. Now left; now right. But though she was completely lost, Celia sensed the little girl knew where she was going and followed her without any argument.

But after a long slow session of burrowing, Celia could tell they were descending quite steeply. That meant they were heading farther away from any chance of rescue and she didn't want to do that. The sound of digging above them grew fainter; then faded altogether. Celia stopped crawling and grasped the little girl's ankle.

"Why're we going down?" she asked as the child looked back at her. "We should be going *up*." When the little girl didn't seem to understand her, Celia pointed downward and shook her head, no. Then she pointed upward and nodded, yes.

The little girl shook her head, no, and pointed downward.

She then crawled through a small opening between two slabs of concrete and disappeared in the gloom ahead. Celia hesitated, reluctant to follow. The face of the little girl reappeared in the opening. She beckoned for Celia to follow her. Celia pointed upward and said, first in Spanish and then in English, "This way. People digging. Trying to find us." Without waiting for the little girl to answer, or shake her head, Celia sat up and pulled on a large broken piece of plasterboard blocking their way overhead. Instantly, it came loose and fell on Celia's head. Stunned, she wasn't able to move out of the way of several more pieces of plasterboard that came crashing down on top of her.

When the dust cleared, Celia lay half-buried under a pile of debris. Terrified, she struggled to extricate herself. It took a few minutes and by the time she could sit up and look about her, she realized the little girl was gone. A wave of panic raced through her. She sensed she had chased away her only hope of being saved. She clutched the tiny silver crucifix that hung from a chain around her neck, kissed it and begged God to make the little girl come back.

When she didn't, Celia decided to at least follow the little girl's directions. She crawled through the small opening ahead of her. But instead of salvation, a blank wall faced her. Her heart sank. Then a large rat ran, squeaking, over her bare leg. She gasped and shrank back. Her nerve broke. She buried her face in her hands and sobbed.

A small brown hand, the flesh of which had been badly blistered by fire, tapped her on the shoulder. Celia jumped, startled, and through her tears saw the little girl smiling at her. Relieved, Celia smiled back.

"I-I'm sorry I didn't trust you," she said. "Please… go ahead, lead the way. I'll follow."

The little girl turned and crawled alongside the blank wall for a few feet. Then she paused, looking back to make sure Celia was following. Satisfied she was, the little girl pulled up a broken piece of flooring and crawled into a hole. Celia did the same. She found herself crawling down a short steep slope that ended at a flight of stone steps. Below, the little girl stood at the bottom of the steps, waiting for Celia to join her. When Celia did, the little girl continued on along a narrow passage that had manmade adobe walls. Celia followed, eyes wide with amazement. Ahead, an old hand-hewn door was ajar. Light came from the room beyond. They entered the room, which was lighted by several candles burning in metal wall-brackets. Celia saw racks of large wooden barrels all around her and realized she was in some kind of ancient wine cellar.

"What is this place?" she asked, looking about her. When there was no answer, Celia turned to repeat her question to the little girl and realized she was no longer there. There was no other exit and Celia wondered where she'd gone. She looked behind all the wine barrels, but found no one. Cobwebs hung everywhere and there was a strong dank musty smell that suggested the cellar hadn't been used in a long time. Dust whitened the tops of the barrels. Celia rubbed away some of the dust on one barrel and saw a small plaque underneath. There was printing on it. It was in Spanish and when Celia read it, she realized that the wine in this barrel had been a gift to the San Fernando Mission from Father Fermin Lasuen. It was a name she'd learned about in her California history class. She remembered he was the friar who'd taken over after the founder of missions, Father Serra, died. Confused, she wondered how she could have crawled from under her apartment building to the old partly-restored mission, which was more than a block away. She couldn't have, she knew, and yet… ?

Something white caught her eye in the far corner of the cellar. Curious, she walked toward it. As she got close, she realized what it was and jumped back with a horrified scream.

⋯⊷⊶⋯   ⋯⊷⊶⋯

Teams of rescue workers dug for three days in an effort to find Celia Chavez. By then, thanks to television, most of America knew about the little Mexican girl trapped under the collapsed apartment building. Prayers and messages of hope went out to the Chavez family; especially when a leaking gas main exploded and firemen had to fight long and hard to extinguish the fire that raged through the rubble.

Once the fire was out, excavation continued. Volunteers came from all over the city to help with the digging. Groups of compassionate *Angelinos* brought food and blankets to the various temporary shelters set up by the city for the families made homeless by the earthquake. Local churches were filled with men, women and children all praying for Celia's rescue. A candlelight vigil was held at the mission. Theresa Chavez attended it with her two sons. She begged her husband to come with them. But Rosario refused. He had to keep digging, he said. And no one could make him change his mind. Hour after hour, day after day, he attacked the rubble like a man possessed. "My Celia, she is still alive," he told anyone who tried to take the pick from his blistered hands. "I know it, just as I know my heart is beating."

But now, on the morning of the fourth day after the quake, even Rosario had to admit that the chances of anyone surviving for this long while buried under tons of rubble were remote at best. But he kept digging, digging and hoping, digging and praying that somehow, against all odds, his beloved Celia was still alive.

Just before lunchtime, Rosario collapsed from exhaustion. Mobile television cameras showed him being carried to a nearby rest station. "We should all take a lesson from this man's courage and indomitable spirit," one announcer told his viewers. "He has shown us what it takes to be a loving father."

A local building contractor was moved by the announcer's statement. He took one of his giant earth-movers off a site he was excavating, had a driver bring it to the collapsed apartment building and began moving the mountain of rubble. It was a fine gesture, and it got him a lot of favorable publicity, but no one really believed it would save Celia. It was too late for that. All the experts agreed that even if she hadn't been crushed to death by the collapse of the building, there was no way she could survive for over seventy-two hours without food, water or, most important of all, air, while being buried under tons of debris.

And as the day wore on and evening approached, officials running the rescue operation announced all digging would stop once it got dark.

As is often the case in such tragic but highly newsworthy events, the last hour of digging took on historic proportions. A huge crowd gathered behind the police cordon. Television crews from the local networks kept their cameras taping non-stop as the final minutes ticked off. And newscasters, their voices choked with emotion, kept their anxious viewers tuned in by cutting back and forth from the studio to the digging site.

But when darkness fell, and the digging stopped, Celia still had not been rescued. All cameras focused on Rosario and Theresa Chavez, who stood weeping nearby. Microphones were thrust into their tear-stained faces and eager TV reporters callously begged them to express their feelings at this moment. Theresa buried her face in her hands and turned away. Rosario tried to answer but he couldn't stop crying; and for several agonizing seconds millions upon millions of sympathetic viewers about the country cringed as they watched this brave, exhausted, heart-broken father with the bloody, blistered hands and indomitable spirit stand there weeping uncontrollably.

Then, at the end of that unforgettable moment, it happened: one of the rescue workers shouted that he'd heard a child's voice crying out from the rubble. Instantly, every floodlight and camera was pointed at the spot where the man was now frantically digging. Other diggers ran to help him. Rosario pushed his way through them, grabbed a pick and began digging alongside them.

As he dug, he kept screaming his daughter's name.

But Celia never replied.

His hopes of rescuing her again faded.

Then, to everyone's surprise, the diggers uncovered a flight of old stone steps that led down to an ancient hand-carved door. The door was open and as the men flashed their lights into the dark room beyond, they saw Celia lying face-down in a puddle of wine that dripped from the spigot of one of the barrels.

She was unconscious and, doctors would say later, close to death. They also agreed that in her comatose condition, there was no way she could have called for help. But if Celia didn't cry out, who did? Certainly not the skeleton of the four-year-old child they found sprawled in a corner of the mission wine cellar. And since everyone else who lived in the collapsed apartment building had been accounted for—the mystery was never solved.

As for Celia, when she'd recovered enough to talk, she never mentioned the little Indian girl who'd saved her life. She knew no one would believe her; and besides, she wasn't sure herself that she hadn't imagined the whole thing. After all, how could a skeleton—even a skeleton wearing the same beaded doeskin dress—become a live little girl long enough to lead her to safety and then change back to being a skeleton? It was impossible, Celia was convinced of that. Yet it seemed so real. And how else could she have found her way into the old wine cellar? She wrestled with the dilemma for many weeks; but the image of the little Indian girl refused to go away. Every night she haunted Celia's dreams. And though she never spoke, Celia somehow understood the little girl's thoughts and knew she wanted to be buried next to her father.

Finally, the little girl's pleading got too much for Celia and she went to her priest and confessed everything. The priest listened quietly. Knowing the terrible ordeal Celia had gone through he wasn't surprised that she was having nightmares. But he was too kind and understanding to brush her off. Instead, he advised her to check out the mission library. Perhaps she would find something in the records that would help her. It wasn't the answer Celia had expected, but he was her priest so she did as he suggested. There, in one of the official diaries that recorded the daily events at the mission two centuries ago, she read about the devastating earthquake that on December 21st, 1812, destroyed most of the original compound which in those days covered many acres. Besides causing most of the buildings to collapse, the narrative continued, the earthquake also started a fire. The fire spread to the surrounding hovels belonging to the local Indians who worked for the mission. It was eventually put out and in the end only one hundred-and-sixty Indian converts were burned to death, one of them being the chief's daughter, a four-year-old mute whose body was never recovered.

✠

The Gun

Before you beat a child, be sure you yourself are not the cause of the offense.

– Austin O'Malley

Yesterday morning, a security guard was gunned down during a bank robbery in North Hollywood. There were plenty of witnesses and, for once, all agreed on what the suspect looked like: a tall slim black man with cropped hair, late-twenties, wearing wraparound dark glasses, sporting a mustache and a small goatee, dressed in black jeans, white sneakers and a purple-and-gold Lakers' jacket. Oh, yeah, and one eyewitness was sure the guy drove away in a late-model bronze Camaro with a banged-up right front fender.

With this kind of detailed description, it didn't take the police long to locate the car and round up the robber. But then the case, the kind of case the police refer to as a "no-brainer", began to unravel. For starters, the man wasn't a man at all, but a woman, a tall, statuesque woman in her mid-twenties who freely admitted she was a lesbian. Nor was she black, she was a mulatto with blue eyes and blond hair and skin the color of café latte. Last but not least, she wasn't an American; she was a Cuban with a Green Card and no prior arrests. And though the two robbery-detail detectives (their confidence somewhat shaken by now) made a thorough search of her apartment and the trunk of her car—which was bronze all right, but a Pontiac Firebird, not its look-alike twin, a Camaro—they could find no trace of her disguise or the clothing witnesses had described. Nor could they find the stolen money, or the gun she allegedly used to shoot the security guard. Also, witnesses in the bank all swore the robber talked like a rapper; whereas the young woman spoke very little English and what few words she did know, were mangled by her heavy Cuban accent.

But, oh boy, could she speak Spanish. In fiery tones she angrily informed the Hispanic detectives, Rodriguez and Garcia, that no matter what evidence they found (they hadn't found any), she could not have been the robber, because at the time of the robbery, she was next door getting her nails done in The Clip Joint, a Vietnamese-owned manicure shop. This, she added, her voice dripping contempt, in case they didn't have brains enough to realize, explained why an eyewitness claimed to have seen a bronze Camaro pulling out of the mini-mall parking lot. Because, coincidentally, moments after the robbery, her nails became dry enough for her to drive and she left the shop and drove home.

The by-now-thoroughly-demoralized detectives, red-faced and sweating with humiliation, could only apologize and withdraw with what little dignity was left them; which wasn't a hell of a lot.

Later that same day, the blonde Cuban woman, whose name was Cecile Chaviano, made a telephone call to a motel room in nearby Sherman Oaks. Her lover, Mariel Gaspar, answered. She was three years older than Cecile, had dark skin and cropped black hair, but resembled Cecile in every other way. She'd been smuggled into Miami by her uncle as a teenager and had taught herself to speak American without a detectable Cuban accent.

"How'd it go?" she asked in Spanish. Then, when Cecile had told her everything, she laughed and said: "Is America a great country or what?"

"The banks are easy, too," Cecile said. "How much did we get?"

"Almost seven thousand bucks."

Cecile whistled softly. "And the disguise and Lakers' jacket, you got rid of them like you promised?"

"I burned the mustache and goatee and buried the clothing under some bushes in the park."

"And the gun – what'd you do with that?"

"Ditched it in the wash."

"Was that a smart thing to do? What if someone finds it?"

"So they find it? So, what? The serial numbers are filed off. The handgrips are homemade. The barrel's been cut down. And there're a million other .38 Specials that could be made to look exactly like it. Stop worrying, CeeCee. I got everything covered. We're home free."

Cecile didn't answer for a moment. She adored Mariel and knew she'd die if anything bad ever happened to her.

"You have to teach me to drive better," she said finally.

"Why? You did great."

"I was worried to death the whole time you were hiding in the trunk."

"Why, baby? No one saw me get into it."

"I don't mean that," Cecile said. "When I was driving out of the mall and up Lankershim, I mean. You know what a terrible driver I am. I just knew I was going to have an accident—hit someone and then you'd be hurt or—or even killed."

"Baby, you let me worry about that," Mariel said. "As long as this plan works, we're gonna stick to it."

The gun remained hidden for almost two months. Then, the first of the winter rains came. It rained hard for two straight days, flooding the Valley streets and filling the concrete wash with two feet of fast-flowing water. As it churned along, the water dislodged the rocks covering the gun that Mariel had hidden there on the day of the robbery.

Early the next morning, Saturday, two small boys found the gun while looking for frogs in the wash. The boys, Matt, aged seven, and Aaron, aged six, were best friends who'd lived next door to one another since birth. But this was a gun, man, a real gun, and they both wanted it badly.

"I picked it up first," Matt said.

"Yeah, but I *saw* it first," said Aaron. "If I hadn't seen it, you'd'a never knowed it was there."

"Yes-I-would."

"No-you-wouldn't."

"Would."

"Wouldn't."

The argument continued heatedly for several minutes. Then Matt, who was bigger than Aaron, tried to grab the gun from his friend's hand.

Aaron jumped back, avoiding Matt's grasp, and in so doing accidently pulled the trigger. The bullet hit Matt in the chest, slamming him backward onto the ground. His body rolled down the steep concrete slope and landed in the shallow murky water.

He was dead before the echo of the gunshot faded away.

✠

Spare the Children

The sweetest roamer is a boy's young heart.

– George Edward Woodberry

The boy lay motionless on the floor of the closet. He was in the same position in which he'd collapsed after the whipping: on his stomach, limbs askew, one cheek pressed flat against the hard wooden floor. He felt no pain. He was beyond pain; beyond even numbness. Mercifully, even before the first lash of his uncle's belt struck the welts and scars that already disfigured his bare back, his brain had retreated into a state of oblivion, shutting itself down so that the six-year-old boy's senses were protected from any further brutality.

The boy, Noel Gentry, had no idea how long he'd lain there. It could as well have been minutes as hours. Long ago, he'd lost all sense of time. All sense of days, weeks or months, too. There was just life in the hot, foul-smelling, almost suffocating darkness of the locked closet, nothing else; endless periods of twenty-four hours broken up only by his Aunt Violet's occasional visits when she unlocked the door and begrudgingly handed him food—"Here, eat, you little bastard"—burned toast or oatmeal in the morning, and the left-over scraps of what she and her husband had eaten for dinner in the evening. If she remembered, or felt like it, she would sometimes let him out long enough to run to the bathroom; if she didn't, he was forced to use the old lidless saucepan she'd thrown at him one day when he'd dared to ask how his sister was. At first, the overpowering stench of urine and human feces in that confining space had made him vomit; now, months later, he was used to it and, like the constant whippings, blanked it out.

Lying there on the floor, Noel slowly realized he'd turned his head. He hadn't asked it to turn. He hadn't even felt it turn; hadn't felt any movement at

13

all. But he knew it was turned because now when he opened his eyes, instead of facing the wall he saw the outline of the closet door. His throat was dry. He could barely swallow. He licked his lips. They were swollen and caked with dried blood at the corners. He had vague visions of being in another room with his uncle's fists pounding him. Then everything went blank and he was back in the familiar silent darkness that he knew was the closet. Inches from his nose, no light showed through the crack under the door. His dazed mind processed the information slowly. Finally, it dawned on him that it must be night outside and the bedroom light wasn't turned on.

So, he thought, she's in the dark too. Only her darkness is worse than mine, much worse, because at least I can move around. All she can do is breathe. And blink her eyes and lick her lips. The rest of her was pinned in by the sides of the tight-fitting box. He remembered this from the one time that his aunt had forgotten to lock the closet door after feeding him and he'd waited until her slow, heavy, fat-bodied footsteps plodded downstairs and then crept out into the bedroom and saw the box for the first time; thinking, *Coffin, it's a—*

But then, as he continued to stand there, blinking owlishly in the sunlight shining through the barred window, he saw the two small breathing holes cut out of the top and realized it was in fact a plain wooden box with a hinged lid and a lockable clasp, large enough for a ten-year-old girl to lie down in and small enough to be pushed under the old brass bed in the corner of the room. Memory told him his grandfather and his father had slept in that bed as boys and he, Noel, was expected to sleep in it until he grew up and then passed it on to his son.

Noel Gentry hadn't always lived in a closet; and his sister, Katie, hadn't always been locked in a box. But that had been so long ago there were times when he wondered if it had ever really happened, or if he were just imagining it, like he imagined so many other things happening in order to fill up the endless days spent alone in the closet.

Memory-blurred-by-fantasy distantly remembered a life of happiness, *of white china horses with gold-painted manes and hollow green frogs filled with pink bubblegum and frosty skies full of fleecy clouds made of blueberry banana splits. Two happy, laughing children all bundled up, noses tingling cold and their breath blowing whitely before them, playing in the snowy garden behind their parents' red brick house on the outskirts of St. Paul, Noel helping his sister build a snowman with black-button eyes, a cork nose and glistening red Christmas cherries for its mouth, the two of them trying to stifle their giggling as they sneaked into the tobacco-smelling study and stole Grampa's favorite pipe and stuck it in the snowman's mouth.*

Oh my, their mother had said. Now you've really done it. Grampa will cut off your ears for this.

Grampa, not really angry but growling like a trapped grizzly. Im gonna get you now, ha-ha. Gotta catch us first! Run, run! The two of them laughing and screaming as they scrambled away from his grasping, outstretched hands.

Help, help! A mean old bear is after us!

Grrrrrr, grrrrrr!

And then in summer (or what passed for summer in this wintry land of ten thousand lakes), those few rare warm sunny days squeezed between Minnesota's brittle-leafed red gold autumn and freezing white winter, picking wild blueberries in the woods and lugging the overflowing baskets back home so mom could make jam to wolf down with melting butter on hot flaky homemade biscuits.

Afternoons, with his dad suddenly out of work. Cutbacks or no cutbacks, they got no right to fire a man after almost twenty years of loyal service, 'specially when he's just two months away from getting his pension!

Dont worry, Hank. With all your experience you'll soon find another job.

I don't know, Emma. At my age it doesn't look good. Everybody's hiring young folks, no-nothin' kids they don't have to pay high wages to. I tell you, Emma, it's sad. Seniority ain't a blessing anymore, it's a curse.

His sister picking him up—Oh, you weigh a ton now—and sitting him on the old cracked and weathered swing that hung by two long ropes from the big oak tree whose leafy green canopy shaded the rickety front porch where they all sat in the early evening with insects buzzing and moths banging against the screen-door. Everyone drinking tall, cold glasses of lemonade, Katie pushing him higher and higher till he felt he was kicking the sky.

Not too high, honey, their mother warned, or he'll fall and hurt himself. He's only a little boy, you know.

Oh, momma, stop worrying. He's not gonna fall, are you Nolie?

No. Push me higher! C'mon, Katie, higher, higher!

No, he thought suddenly, *that's wrong.*

The swing wasn't in St. Paul, it was here, in Tulare. Or was it? No, maybe it was in St. Paul after all.

Noel realized he couldn't be sure about what part of his life happened in Minnesota and what happened after they moved out to California. Two formerly separate phases of his life had now permanently blurred into one; a perpetual brain-fade caused not only by incessant beatings and torturings with lighted cigarettes, but helped along by a vivid imagination that he no longer controlled and which was now running rampant, making it impossible for him to separate truth from invention. All he had to do to escape from the locked closet was close his eyes and at once he was free to fly anywhere he wanted, where there was no pain, no hunger, no Uncle Mace or Aunt Vi, only himself, his sister and his parents, now alive again, and all living happily ever after.

Now, in his mind, he forgot about the swing and remembered that the small rundown house they'd rented from Uncle Mace also had a porch, this one in back, the screen on the door rusty and torn so that right after they moved in his father had to fix it before they all were eaten alive by mosquitoes. His mother had said, "For what your tightwad brother's charging us to live in this horrible little shack, you'd think he'd at least pay to have the screens fixed," and the father, not wanting to upset her further, saying in his gentle, placid voice, "Now, Emma, let's not get into that again. But for Mace and Vi, we'd still be in St. Paul and I'd still be looking for work."

"Work!" she'd snorted. "A grown man of your experience, picking avocados for minimum wage! I don't call that work, I call it slave labor!"

"Well, 'least we're eating regular again, and we're all living under the same roof. That's something to be thankful for."

No swing. There was definitely no swing here in Tulare.

Noel was sure of it now. Just a back porch that needed painting and his mother, weak and sickly from the illness no one would talk about in front of him, but still trying to be cheerful as she brought out a big pitcher of fresh tart lemonade that was made, she announced proudly, from lemons growing in their very own backyard! Who would've ever thunk it.

His concerned father leaping up, saying, "Emma, what're you doing? You shouldn't be carrying that, it's way too heavy. Here, let me," and the mother, who came from hardy pioneer stock but now was frail as a butterfly, protesting, "Don't be silly, Hank dear, I can handle it fine," but then setting the heavy pitcher down awkwardly on the table, lemonade spilling onto the cloth. "Oh my goodness, now look what I've done," and Katie jumping up, saying, "Don't worry, momma, I'll get a cloth," and running inside the house.

Memory also recalled that awful day when his mother, now bed-ridden, didn't know who he was when he carried her lunch tray into the bedroom.

My, what a nice little boy you are. So kind of you to bring me my soup.

Be careful, Mom, it's hot.

What's your name, young man? Do you live next door?

Mom, it's me, Noel.

Noel, she repeated dreamily. What a lovely name. It means Christmas, you know.

Remembering, too, how he couldn't wait to get out of the room; and later, when his sister found him crying in the bathroom, and he'd sobbed out what had happened, she put her arms around him and hugged him so tightly he could barely breathe, saying, "It's all right, Nolie. I'm here now. I'll protect you. Shhh, don't cry—"

"But she don't even know who I am!"

"I know. Sometimes she doesn't know who I am, either. Or daddy. But you mustn't let it upset you. She still loves us. It's just that she's ill and can't always remember everything."

Her condition quickly worsened. Soon she couldn't remember anything, not even how to dress herself. Then, one spring day, she mercifully forgot how to breathe. Even though they expected it, it was still a shock.

You know, his father said trying to ease their pain. In a way we should be glad she's gone. Put her out of her misery. Poor mother suffering like that.

They called the mortician, a short plump gloomy man in a shiny black suit who came and waited patiently while a minister said loving words over her.

God in all His glory loved her, and now she's with Him forever, waiting for us to join her.

Noel was puzzled. If God loved mom why'd he make her suffer? Hush, his father said. Shhhh, said his sister. Noel fell silent, wondering why whenever he questioned God's motives somebody always shut him up.

Then her body was carried out to the awaiting hearse and brother and sister watched as their mother, a sweet, gentle, loving woman who'd never struck them or even raised her voice in anger, was driven off to be prepared for burial in the local cemetery.

The kitchen was his favorite room in the house. Which house I don't know. Wish I could remember. A bright, cheerful room with yellow floral wallpaper and brown linoleum with potted geraniums growing in the window. Always warm and full of different wonderful smells; cooking stewed apples for dad's birthday or turkey with gravy and biscuits on Sunday. A lemon pie for Katie with a crunchy graham cracker crust and the meringue so fluffy and thick you couldn't take a bite without getting it stuck all around your mouth, like a white beard.

Look momma, Nolie looks like Santa Claus.

After the funeral, Noel realized, his father changed. Almost overnight he started drinking whiskey from a silver flask he kept hidden in his hip pocket.

Stumbling drunkenly about the house, knocking things over, yelling why the hell did we ever come to this godforsaken hole Tulare? Who ever heard of Tulare, for chrissake? I doubt if it's even on the map!

Collapsing on the couch, passing out, his cigarette burning down between his big-knuckled fingers.

Please, daddy, wake up! You'll burn the house down one day if—

It got steadily worse. He lost his temper for no reason and yelled at his children, something he'd never done while his wife was alive. He worked only when he felt like it and got into shouting matches with his brother, who told him if he wasn't going to work, then to get his lazy ass and his two ugly brats off the property.

What happened next, Noel and Katie would remember for the rest of their lives: they were suddenly awakened in the middle of the night by a single gunshot; and when they rushed into their father's bedroom, they found him sprawled on the floor beside the bed. He was dead, his face twisted into an eternal grimace, the blood rushing from a gaping hole in his temple.

Please forgive me, his note read, but I'm just too weak and full of pain inside to go on living without her. Try not to hate me too much, Love always, Dad

Their father was buried next to his beloved wife. Shortly after that Noel and Katie were taken before a judge. He looked frighteningly stern in his long black robe, but he treated them kindly, his voice gentle and understanding as he asked them if they would like to be adopted by their aunt and uncle. Noel, about to say yes, stopped as his sister nudged him and stood up.

"What happens to us, sir, if we don't want to be adopted?"

"Then you become wards of the state," the judge said. "What that means is, you'll be put into foster homes until you're both old enough to live by yourselves."

Uncle Mace's lawyer, who sat beside Katie and up till now hadn't said much, placed his hand over hers as if to advise her to keep quiet. Katie ignored him.

"Together, or separate?"

"Together, if possible—"

"Then, we don't want to be adopted," Katie said quickly.

"Let me finish, young lady," the judge continued. "I said, *if possible*. But I can't guarantee it. The court will try its best to keep you two together, but there's a definite chance that you might have to live apart. Perhaps not even in the same area. Do you both understand that?"

Katie nodded. She looked at her aunt and uncle, who sat glaring in their seats behind her, then at Noel sitting beside her. He knew that for reasons she wouldn't discuss, she'd never liked Uncle Mace or Aunt Violet, but he hadn't realized until now that she disliked them enough to consider living with strangers in a foster home. And maybe not even the same foster home as her brother. The idea terrified him. He wanted to speak up, to tell Katie and the judge that he wanted to be adopted. But he trusted her. She was the one rock in his life that never crumbled; never let him down. So he waited, silent, teeth chewing nervously on his lip, face uplifted to hers, until he saw tears welling into her eyes; felt her hand clasp his.

"Okay," Katie told the judge. "They can adopt us."

No one spoke on the long hot dusty drive back to the avocado ranch. The four of them sat, adults in front, children in back, riding along like sweating statues. Twice Noel thought of speaking, but each time his sister squeezed his hand harder and shook her head, so he kept silent. But he did notice his uncle glaring at them in the rearview mirror. Noel had never seen eyes filled with such intense hatred. He was puzzled. He wondered what could have made his uncle so angry. It wasn't until later, when the four of them were in the cool, air-conditioned, beam-ceilinged living room of the ranch-house, that Noel learned the reason:

"You're gonna be sorry, both of you," Uncle Mace told them. He spoke through gritted teeth, black eyes glaring, his big club-like fists clenched at his sides. "By the time I get through with you, you'll wish you'd never been born."

"Why?" Noel said. "What'd we do?"

"You know goddamn well what you did," Uncle Mace said, answering Noel but looking directly at Katie. "Humiliating your Aunt Violet and me in front of everyone, way you did in court. Think I won't get even for that?"

"Go ahead. You can't scare me." Katie thrust her jaw out defiantly. "I ain't afraid of you and neither's little Nolie, here."

"Reckon we'll see about that," Uncle Mace said.

"Oh, don't waste your breath on them," Aunt Violet told her husband. "Ungrateful little bastards, the pair of 'em. They can rot in hell, for all I care."

⊷≔⊚   ⊚≔⊶

The beatings and burnings with hot objects didn't happen right away. At first, nothing happened at all. Days went by. It was the picking season. Uncle Mace was busy recruiting the numerous impoverished families of itinerant Mexicans that followed the seasons throughout the state, picking one crop after another, living on ranches and farms in hovels that had no running water and only dirty straw mattresses to sleep on.

Meanwhile, Aunt Violet kept the books, such as they were, making sure she paid the lowest wages possible and threatening to fire anyone who complained. She was a big, pink, fleshy woman who looked even bigger in bright-colored Hawaiian *mu-mus* that she bought from a mail-order catalog. She idolized Tammy Faye Baker. She watched her whenever she was on the religious channel and also on video tapes that Aunt Vi mailed away for. She mimicked Tammy's every movement, wearing her dyed-blonde hair similarly frizzed out and her false eyelashes dripping with so much mascara, they left tracks on her cheeks. But she also had habits of her own. She bit her nails until they bled, covering them with fake porcelain tips whenever she drove to town; she also smoked incessantly, chain-lighting one cigarette from another, always keeping the cigarette dangling in the left corner of her crimson mouth, so that by the time she reached thirty, her cheek was stained yellow by the up-curling smoke.

Katie hated her, perhaps even more than she hated Uncle Mace. *Aunt Vi's evil,* she told Noel. *Y'mean like Doctor Doom?* he said. *Worse. She's treacherous. She smiles all the time, and pretends to be nice and friendly and religious, but inside she's mean and hateful and there isn't anything she wouldn't do to hurt us.*

"She'd better not try anything," Noel said darkly, "or I'll tell Uncle Mace on her."

Katie looked at him, realizing that in his five-year-old mind he didn't truly understand the situation.

"Don't do that," she warned. "Uncle Mace won't help you."

"Why not?"

"'Cause he's worse."

→▷◁—   —▷◁←

Once the Mexican pickers were hired, Uncle Mace had more time to think about revenge. In his mean, hate-fermented brain he worked out a long-range plan that started with a trip to the lumberyard, where he bought enough wood to make a five-foot-long box. He told no one why he was making the box, though he sensed his wife would like his idea. During the twenty-odd years they'd been married, she'd often shown him that she had a sadistic streak. It had started with the time she'd offered to drown the litter of puppies that her dog, Shep, had given birth to under the porch.

Up till then he hadn't known just how cruel his wife could be, although he'd had his suspicions. So he'd told her to go ahead, and he had watched her do just that, a dark sense of sexual arousal growing in him all the while.

Afterwards they'd had the best sex ever.

After the coffin-like box was made, Mace hid it in the barn. Then, on Friday, when his wife went to town to have her toenails painted, he dragged the box upstairs into the spare bedroom and slid it under the bed; the brass bed that he'd always wanted but that his father had willed to his older brother, Hank.

God, how he hated Hank. Smarter, stronger, better-looking and always everybody's favorite, Hank got all the breaks in life, while Mace was treated like the black sheep. One day, he'd promised himself as he sat alone in his room, listening to his family and their friends singing *Happy Birthday* to Hank, he swore he'd get even for all the injustices he'd endured.

And now that day had come; he was getting back at Hank; at everyone. His only regret was that Hank and his sweeter-than-molasses former prom-queen wife weren't still alive to see what Uncle Mace had planned for their cute little smart-ass daughter.

He'd intended to keep his plan a secret for awhile; at least until most of the pieces were in place. But that night in bed, his wife had refused to let him go to sleep until he told her what was going on in his demented brain. *You're not fooling me,* she said when he didn't answer. *I know you, remember? You got something cooking up there and I want to know about it—right now.*

What if you don't like it? he said.

Oh, I'm sure I will, she assured him. *And if it's got something to do with them two snot-nosed kids, like I think it has, you'll probably need my help.*

Truth was, he did. So, he told her. Everything. Right down to the smallest detail. He spoke slowly, eyes half-glazed over, voice hoarse with passion, embellishing the parts he liked best, knowing he'd get a sexual rush by just talking about it. Violet, enjoying herself along with him, listened without once interrupting him. Then, when he was finished, she sat straight up in bed, her left eye squinted as the smoke from her cigarette drifted up into it, and stared at him in fond admiration.

"My God," she said. "All this time, honeybunch, I've sorely underestimated you."

Mace smiled, pleased by her flattery.

Katherine "Katie" Gentry knew exactly how long she'd been locked in the box: eight months and fourteen days now. And counting. Unlike her brother, who rarely left the closet, Katie was let out every day for a couple of hours and forced to be Aunt Vi's slave. Hobbled by ankle chains so she couldn't run away, she ironed, scrubbed floors, washed dishes, vacuumed—did whatever menial chore her aunt ordered her to do. And if she didn't do them to her aunt's satisfaction—which was governed by mood swings that fluctuated every day—she was punished. At first, Aunt Violet merely beat her with a broken broom handle. But as time passed, a simple beating no longer satisfied Aunt Vi's sadistic nature, and that's when the torturing started.

Katie had just finished ironing some sheets and was putting them away when her aunt entered and erupted because of the way Katie had folded them. She grabbed the hot iron, pushed Katie face-down on the kitchen table and pressed the plate onto her back. Katie was only wearing a skimpy t-shirt, and her skin sizzled. She screamed and fought to get loose, but it was hopeless. A skinny ten-year-old, Katie was outweighed by two hundred pounds. By the time her aunt let her go, Katie had passed out from the pain caused by several burns.

Her screaming brought Uncle Mace running in from the barn. When he entered the kitchen and saw Katie sprawled on the floor, her back one big raw blister, he had only one comment:

"Next time, sugar, let me watch, okay?"

From then on the beatings and burnings were a common occurrence. Scissors heated on the gas stove, cigarettes, fists, the heel of her aunt's shoe—all were used to inflict pain on Katie. Uncle Mace never touched her; he got his enjoyment from watching. Eyes glazed, teeth chewing on his knuckles, he'd stand there writhing in ungodly ecstasy, faint animal whimpers coming from him.

And through it all, Katie never uttered a sound. She'd made up her mind after the first burning that no matter how badly it hurt, she wasn't going to give her aunt or uncle the pleasure of hearing her scream. So she accepted the torture, somehow finding the strength not to cry out—even though she knew that her silence only goaded her aunt into inflicting even more pain.

Escape was always uppermost in her mind. And though she knew her chances of getting away were remote, she never gave up on the idea. It was in fact one of two things that kept her alive. The other was her brother. She knew she was his only hope of escaping as well, because no one outside the house would ever help them. Her aunt and uncle had made sure of that by notifying the school and all their neighbors that Katie and Noel had gone back to Minnesota to live. "We hated to see the little darlings go," Katie heard Aunt Vi telling someone on the phone. "But we felt we had to do what was best for them. Poor dears were never really happy here, you know. Even when their parents, God bless them, were alive. They missed their friends and the rural atmosphere they grew up in."

Winter came. Snow and icy winds hit the region. It wasn't as cold as Minnesota, but it was cold enough to threaten the crops. Nightly, as Katie lay there trapped in the box, she heard her brother shivering and coughing in the closet. "He's sick," she kept telling her aunt. "He needs a doctor."

"And of course I'll make sure he gets one," Aunt Vi said, mockingly.

"He'll die if you don't," Katie said. "Then you'll both be murderers."

"Now that really worries me," said her aunt. She swung her big meaty fist and punched Katie alongside her ear, knocking her sprawling. "Now, get your lazy ass downstairs and wash them pots'n pans!"

That night, Noel's coughing and wheezing got worse. Katie, confined in the box, broke one of her aunt's cardinal rules ("I ever hear either one'a you talking to each other, I'll beat you to a pulp!") and called out to her brother. Noel didn't reply. Katie wondered if he hadn't heard her or was too sick to speak. Tomorrow, she thought, she had to find a way to call the doctor. But, how? There was no phone in the room and the one downstairs in the parlor had a lock on it. *Please God,* she prayed, *help me find a way to get a doctor so poor Nolie doesn't die.*

The next morning, Friday, was ironing day. At eight-fifteen Aunt Vi came laboring upstairs and let Katie out of the box. She then locked her left ankle to the chain that was fastened around the heavy brass bed and pointed a fat finger at the pile of clean but wrinkled clothes she'd brought up. "I want everything ironed 'fore nine o'clock," she said. "And not one second after, you hear?"

Katie nodded. She knew every Friday her aunt had a nine-thirty appointment to get her toenails painted, and she tried desperately to think of a way she could use this time out of the box to escape or get to a phone. But no idea came to her. And all the time, Noel kept coughing until it sounded like his whole chest was breaking apart.

"Hang on, Nolie," Katie whispered to him through the closet door. "Doctor's coming soon. Then you'll be all right."

Noel tried to speak but he was too weak. His wheezing erupted into another coughing spasm.

Katie went to the barred window and looked out. Outside, everything was blanketed with snow. She looked out across the vast white fields and saw in the distance traffic crawling along the Interstate. There were people in those cars; people who'd help her get a doctor. If only she could reach them, signal them even. But, how? The chain around her ankle didn't even reach to the door. And it was no good thinking of attacking her aunt and stealing the keys Katie knew she kept on a chain around her neck. Aunt Vi may be fat and slow, but she was much stronger than Katie and wouldn't hesitate to beat her senseless. No, her only hope of overpowering her aunt was by surprise. But how in a room whose only furnishings were a brass bed and a wooden box, do you surprise someone; especially someone as suspicious as Aunt Vi?

You don't, Katie realized.

She sighed, depressed and frustrated, and went on ironing. But a few moments later, as she placed a freshly-pressed yellow-and-purple flowered mu-mu on the bed, it hit her. The door!

Quickly, Katie moved to the rear of the bed, put her back against the wall and pushed. The heavy brass bed inched forward. Katie pushed again, harder. The bed moved about a foot. Katie took a deep breath and pushed again. The bed moved another foot or so. Katie paused, wondering if her aunt had heard the bed moving downstairs. When she didn't hear anything, Katie pushed the bed forward a final time and then picked up the chain, so it wouldn't clank, and walked to the door. She was about two feet short. She returned to the bed and pushed it forward until she was satisfied the chain was now long enough to serve her purpose. Then, unplugging the iron, she went and hid behind the open door.

Shortly before nine, Katie heard Aunt Vi laboring up the stairs. Katie fought down her panic and stood perfectly still, iron raised above her head. "You better have them damn clothes ironed," Aunt Vi growled as she entered the room, "or I'l—"

Katie stepped from behind the door and swung the iron with every ounce of strength she possessed. The heavy iron smashed against the back of Aunt Vi's head. She gave a startled grunt of pain, then her knees buckled and she collapsed on the floor. Katie stood there for a moment, stunned by what she'd done. But when her aunt didn't move, Katie quickly kneeled beside her and tried to find the keys. It took a few moments before she found the chain buried among the sweaty bulges of fat that formed her aunt's neck; when she did, she ran her hand along it to the front and jerked the two keys loose. The second key was for the closet. After unlocking the clasp holding the chain to her ankle, Katie ran to the closet and unlocked the door.

The stench of urine and feces made her gag. She held her breath and stepped inside, looking for her brother. Noel was slumped in a corner, too weak to move; to even cough. Katie slipped her arm under him, "C'mon, upsadaisy," and, after a struggle, managed to get him on his feet. He was a ghost of himself, so gaunt and ashen, so frail and sickly, she felt as if she were supporting a skeleton.

Somehow, she got him to the door and, step-by-painful-step, down the stairs into the living room. There, she gently lowered Noel into a chair and began searching for the key to unlock the telephone. She went through all the drawers. No key. Frantic, she checked the liquor cabinet and the coffee table. Nothing. Any moment, she knew Aunt Vi would regain consciousness; or Uncle Mace might step through the front door. Where? Where? Where? The cuckoo clock struck nine-fifteen. As the little wooden bird popped out, chirping the time, Katie's eyes were drawn to the clock. It was then she noticed the tiny drawer at the base. Something told her the key was in there. She hurried to the clock, pulled open the drawer and saw the key inside. Snatching it up, she ran to the old black telephone on the end table beside the couch, unlocked the dial and hurriedly called 911.

"P-Please," she told the operator, "my brother, he needs a doctor."

"Calm down," the operator said. "What's wrong with him?"

"He's sick—got this awful cough—oh please, hurry, he's got to see a doctor! He's been locked in this closet for months and he'll die if he doesn't—"

"All right, all right, give me the address."

As Katie was hanging up, she saw Uncle Mace walking from the barn to the house. Trapped, she ran into the kitchen and grabbed a long-bladed carving knife from the butcher's block. She ran back into the living room with it and stood, like a guard dog, in front of Noel.

When Uncle Mace entered the house and saw Katie standing by her brother, knife in hand, he was so surprised he stopped and stared at her, unable to believe his eyes. "How the hell'd you get out, you little bitch?" He started toward her.

Katie brandished the knife at him. "Don't come any closer, or I'll kill you."

"We'll see about that, girlie." Uncle Mace grabbed a cushion from a chair, held it in front of him like a shield and slowly closed in on Katie.

She slashed at him with the knife. He fended the blade off with the cushion and moved closer. Katie tried to stab him. He jammed the cushion against the blade. As the sharp steel sank in up to the hilt, he wrenched the cushion sideways, tearing the knife out of Katie's hand. She backed up, desperately looking for a weapon. But he was on her too quickly and wrestled her to the floor. Katie bit and kicked and punched, but it was useless. Uncle Mace grabbed her wrists and twisted her arms up behind her back. He then held both wrists with one hand and, cocking back his other fist, punched her in the face. He kept punching, though she was already unconscious, until his sadistic impulses were quenched. Then he stood up, chest heaving, went to the couch and looked at the boy slumped, motionless, against the cushions. Uncle Mace pressed two fingers against Noel's neck. He could feel no pulse. Mercifully, Noel was dead.

Well, now, Uncle Mace thought, *that takes care of one of the little brats.* Eyes glazed, he looked up, heavenward to him, seeing in his fermented mind not the old low beamed-ceiling but the faces of everyone who'd made his childhood so miserable.

"Reckon I've paid you back for some of it," he said.

Just then he heard his wife descending the stairs, cursing every ponderous painful step she made.

⇥⇤

Uncle Mace was returning from behind the barn, where he'd buried Noel's corpse under a pile of snow, when the paramedics arrived. The sight of the red-and-white fire department vehicle pulling up in front of his house shocked him. Only a few minutes ago he'd locked Katie back in the box, and notified the doctor's office that he was bringing his wife in because she'd fallen and hurt her head. So, what were the paramedics doing here?

He quickened his pace, reaching the house before the two paramedics were out of their vehicle, and entered the living room. His wife turned from the window, put a finger over her lips and held up the tiny lock that fitted in the telephone dial.

"I'll handle this," she told him. "You just let 'em in and then shut up."

Uncle Mace gladly obeyed. He never questioned his wife's instructions; in fact, he enjoyed being ordered around by her. It not only relieved him of responsibility, it made him feel safe and protected. And Uncle Mace hadn't felt safe or protected since the day he'd left his mother's womb.

Once the two young muscular paramedics were in the living room, they looked about them, puzzled.

"Where's the little boy who needs a doctor?" one asked.

"Little boy?" Aunt Vi looked at her husband, then back at the paramedics. "Must be some mistake. We got no kids."

"But some young girl called 911 and said—"

"That was me," Aunt Vi said. "Guess I was so hysterical, my voice must've sounded like a young girl's. See, I'd just come to after the fall, so I probably didn't make a lot of sense. I'm sorry if I caused any trouble. But," she paused and turned her head so the paramedics could see all the dried blood in her hair, "as you can see, I'm the one who needs patching up."

The paramedics exchanged questioning looks, then shrugged and opened their medical kits to tend to Aunt Violet's injury.

Upstairs in the box in the spare bedroom, Katie slowly regained consciousness. Her face, swollen and bruised from her uncle's punches, throbbed with pain. Katie didn't care. She'd learned how to handle pain. All that mattered to her now was, she no longer had to worry about her brother. *Thank you God,* she prayed, *for letting Nolie die. Now they can't hurt him anymore. Now he's up there in heaven with You and momma and daddy and Grampa, having a great old time, I'm sure. And you know what, God? I wish You would let me die too, so I could be with them. I know it's wrong to wish I was dead, or to want to kill myself, but I do. Because if I was dead, God, I could be with all the people I love, and then I'd be happy, too.*

✠

Of Kites, Tide Pools and Fireflies

Every child born into the world is a new thought of God, an ever-fresh and radiant possibility.

– Kate Douglas Wiggin

Once a year, after Thanksgiving, I treat myself to a week of relaxation in a time-share condominium located on the bluffs at Del Mar, California. Del Mar is a sleepy, sun-baked little coastal town north of San Diego, known mainly for its racetrack. I don't know when the track was founded, or by whom, but I do know that Bing Crosby and Jimmy Durante were major players. And according to an old screenwriter I know, during racing season in the thirties and forties, all the famous Hollywood celebrities used to drive down to L.A's Union Station, where they boarded a special racetrack train, crowded into the club-car, got happily pie-eyed during the two-hour ride south, and spent the weekend betting at the track whose advertising slogan was, and still is, "Where the turf meets the surf."

This year I was particularly in need of a rest, emotionally and physically, having spent the past three months rewriting a screenplay for a producer who hated every idea I suggested. Now, producers love to make writers crazy, I'm convinced of that, so I and most screenwriters I know have grown somewhat immune (numbed, might be more accurate) to their "minor changes" that always involve altering key characters and restructuring the whole goddamn script; truth is, we'd probably get suspicious if they *didn't* mess with our creations. Being born with a healthy dose of paranoia, we'd know in our hearts that they obviously hated "our baby" and were merely biding their time until we met our contractual obligations so they could fire us and hire the writer they always wanted on the project in the first place.

Anyway, as you can tell, I needed a rest.

The first day I arrived, I did what I always do; tried to wind down. I changed into my old orange surfer trunks, opened a cold Corona, grabbed one of the books I'd been saving specially for this week of doing-absolutely-nothing, and sat in the sun on the walkway fronting the condo. The complex is built along the cliff-tops overlooking the beach, giving each unit giving an un-paralleled view of the ocean. The train tracks run right past the complex, on a slightly lower level, which gives the place a rural mid-western quality I love (is there a more wonderful, adventurous sound than the mournful wail of a train whistle at night?), far out-weighing the briefly annoying feeling that you're experiencing a minor earthquake as every so often a train thunders past.

The condo has a kitchen, so I generally cook in. Then I go to bed early, leaving the windows open, and fall asleep listening to the surf breaking on the beach far below. Contentment and serenity reign. Come mornings, I take long walks along the sand, watching the surfers and all the different breeds of dogs chasing each other and tangling up the legs of their owners on Dog Beach. Then I return home, take a nap, read some more, grab a bite to eat, swig down a cold one, and doze away the day. And as boring as it may sound that is what my annual week of R 'n' R normally consists of.

But this time it was different. On Monday, with the weekend crowd gone, my morning stroll along the beach introduced me to a young girl. She was alone, a tall, slender, leggy girl in a pale yellow bikini, her face hidden by her long sun-streaked hair as she bent over one of the tide pools formed among the rocks near Dog Beach. I guessed she was about twelve or thirteen, an age that has always confused me. I never quite know if I'm dealing with a child or a young woman, or both. As a result, I never know what to say or how to act around them, and end up feeling terribly uncomfortable, as I'm sure they do too. Now this may be a problem only I suffer with, but I don't think so. A female writer I admire once referred to her 13-year-old daugh-ter as being in her own "private *Twilight Zone,* a hellishly turbulent period sometimes lasting throughout the teenage years that all girls must struggle through and survive, when every hormone in their body is exploding in dif-ferent, conflicting directions."

Now, this may be a mother's exaggeration, brought on by her own frus-tration at not being able to deal with her daughter's changing personalities. But it made sense to me and so it was with trepidation that I approached the young girl, intending to skirt the tide pools and thus avoid being drawn into conversation. Because, despite being an introverted bachelor with no chil-dren of my own, kids adore me. It's the same with cats. They seem to know I dislike them and torture me by ignoring their owner's lofty assurances of "Don't worry, she hates strangers; won't even go near them," by promptly hurling themselves into my lap where they curl up and contentedly (mali-ciously, I think) purr themselves to sleep.

Now, kids don't hurl themselves at me, and I try never to let them sleep in my lap, but they do seem to single me out, drawn to me as if I'm a contemporary Pied Piper. Today was no different. As I passed the young girl, she spoke without looking up, said in a low, surprisingly mature voice: "Ever see crabs making out?"

I stopped because, if nothing else, I'm not rude.

"No."

"There," she pointed. "See, right near that tiny rock."

I saw nothing but rocks and greenish cloudy water.

"Too late. They went under the kelp."

"Story of my life," I said. "I'm always out getting popcorn when the good stuff happens."

"Wait," she said as I started to walk on. "I want to ask you something."

"What?"

She now looked up, a small pale oval face that was all eyes, deep-set amber eyes with gold flecks dancing in them, and, below a tiny up-tilted sunburned nose, a wide, full-lipped, sensuous mouth that belonged to a grown woman.

"D'you have any matches?"

"Uh-uh."

Again, I started away. Again, she stopped me.

"I used to live in there."

"Where?"

"This tide pool."

"Really? When was that?"

"'Bout a million years ago… when I was a mermaid."

"Oh."

"Go ahead, laugh all you want."

"I wasn't laughing."

"I don't care if you make fun of me."

"Wasn't making fun of you, either."

"But you don't believe me, do you?"

"Sure. Why would you make up something like that?"

"Here, I'll prove it to you."

She crouched down, reached into the water under the kelp, grabbed something tiny, put it in her mouth and crunched it down.

"See," she said. "Only a mermaid would eat a raw crab."

Now, I'm not normally a queasy guy. But I have to admit my stomach turned over.

"Aren't you impressed?"

"Very," I said. "Now, if the show's over, I'll be moving along."

"Okay if I walk with you?"

I shrugged. "It's a public beach."

"If you don't want me to, I won't." Her wide-eyed, up-tilted face seemed to be mocking me.

"Okay," I said, wishing I'd said no. "But only if you promise not to eat anything that crawls or swims."

"Deal." She raised her left hand for me to high-five. Her fingernails, though badly bitten, were the same bilious blue as her lipstick and toenails. I slapped her palm with mine and we walked on. Ahead, a small boy ran along the water's edge, trailing a red kite that had a yellow Happy Face painted on it.

"That's what I'm coming back as," she said, pointing. "You know, in my next life."

"I can think of worse things," I said. "But, at your age, I'd enjoy this one first."

"How can I?" she said. "When all the time I wish I was dead?"

She certainly knew how to kill a conversation, no pun intended. I watched as she picked up a pebble and threw it in the air, narrowly missing a low-flying seagull. Hoping she hadn't been aiming at the gull, I heard myself say: "Why would you wish that?"

"'Cause... "

"Because, what?"

If she heard me, she didn't show it. She stood there, an incoming wave swirling about her bare feet, staring up at the sky and God only knows what else, seemingly trapped in her thoughts.

"You didn't answer my question," I said.

She came back from somewhere far off, said, ""There's where I live," pointing at a pale blue wood-framed bungalow perched on the low cliffs that faced the ocean. "'Bye."

She ran off. I watched her tall, lanky body race across the sloping sand, knees pumping, long hair streaming out behind her, realizing as I did that I was strangely fascinated by her. When she reached the path that led up to the cliff-tops, she turned and waved at me. Her voice came floating to me on the wind.

"Thanks for rapping with me."

Then she was gone.

⇢▪▣ ▣▪⇠

Later that afternoon, after a long nap in the warm sun, I took another walk along the beach. If you'd asked me if I was hoping to see the young girl again, I would've said no. But I'd've been lying. Much as I tried to deny it to myself, my curiosity was wetted and I wanted to talk to her again; to find out what made her tick and why I found her fascinating. But she wasn't around. Not on the beach, or on the patio of the pale blue bungalow atop the cliffs. Disappointed yet strangely relieved (somehow I sensed she was trouble), I returned to my condo and ate a dinner of salad and cold cuts in front of the television. Then, weary from all the exercise and salt air, I fell asleep on the couch.

I don't remember getting up and putting myself to bed, but I must have because there I was, in bed, in the buff, when I awoke the next morning. I dozed until six-thirty, then got up, put on my shorts and running shoes and headed outside. There's a path in front of my condo that leads down to the beach. There's also a grassy mound with a bench on it for anyone wanting to sit and gaze at the ocean. At night it was occupied by young lovers or old couples holding hands. But early in the morning it was always empty—which was why I was startled when, as I walked past, something stirred. I looked back and saw someone huddled there in a blanket, knees drawn up to their chin, arms clasped about their legs, an old khaki fisherman's hat pulled low over their face. It was alive, I realized, and shivering.

Hoping it wasn't a homeless person (the homeless always make me feel guilty), I moved closer and saw it was the young girl. Her lips were still blue, but now from the cold, not lipstick.

"Boy, you scared the heck out of me. What're you doing here?"

"What's it look like?" she said, peering up at me from under the floppy brim of her hat. "W-Waiting for you."

"How'd you know where I live?"

"I f-followed you. Last night. Didn't see me, d-did you?"

"No." I suppose I should've felt flattered, but for some reason I couldn't put my finger on, I was uneasy and a little irked. "Why'd you do that?"

"W-Wanted to know where you l-lived."

"Could've asked."

"More f-fun this w-way." Her shivering increased.

"How long you been here?"

"Dunno. L-Long time. All n-n-night, maybe."

"All night? No, you're making that up. You can't've been here all—I mean, what about your folks?"

"Mom's the only one h-here and she t-t-takes sleeping pills. Don't be angry," she said, seeing my expression. "I often s-stay out all night. S'only way I get to t-talk to the s-stars."

She was so matter-of-fact about it, I almost believed her. "C-C-Can we go inside?" she said, her teeth clicking as she shivered. "I'm f-f-frigging freezing."

"I don't think that's such a good idea," I said. "At this hour in the morning… me alone… you a young girl… it mightn't look right."

"I p-p-promise not to r-rape you."

"I have a better idea. Why don't I drive you home?"

She reacted as if I'd slapped her. Jumping up, she glared at me, her deep-set amber eyes narrowed with sudden rage.

"B-Bastard!" she hissed at me. "I hate you! Wish you were dead!" And before I could stop her, she ran off along the path.

I was stunned. I'd never seen anyone get so intensely angry without violent provocation. For a moment I considered changing the route of my run. In this insane world of drive-by-shootings and school kids killing each other over sneakers, it wasn't inconceivable that she was hiding somewhere ahead with a gun. Then I quickly dismissed the idea, thinking, *For Chrissake, get a grip, will you? Save your paranoia for your writing.*

My run along the beach was uneventful. The tide was out, leaving the damp sand firm and cool, and the silvery-gray ocean reflected the streaks of pale pink, yellow and green that tinted the cloudless lavender sky.

Exhilarated by my run and the pure joy of being alive on such a glorious day, I'd forgotten all about the incident with the young girl by the time I reached the path leading to the top of the bluff. But as I toiled upward and came within sight of my condo, I was abruptly reminded of it by the sight of her sitting on my doorstep. Her hands were hidden under the blanket draped over her shoulders, and I approached cautiously. But I needn't have worried; as she saw me she smiled, got stiffly to her feet and waved as if we were old friends.

"I bought you some coffee."

She pointed at two Styrofoam cups sitting on the porch chair. "Didn't know if you liked it with or without, so I got both."

"Thanks," I said. "With."

She handed me one of the cups, took the other for herself, and sipped her coffee through the tiny hole in the lid.

"I've stopped shivering, see…" She stretched out a long slender sunburned arm and showed me her hand. She wasn't shivering but she'd been at her bright blue nails again, biting the cuticles bloody.

I started to tell her she shouldn't bite her nails. Then, not wanting risk another flare-up, I said a bit lamely: "I'm glad. Being cold's the pits."

"Fish eggs," she said, making it sound like *Up Yours.*

"Be nice, now."

"Then, don't talk down to me. My folks are always doing that and I hate it. I may be young but I'm not stupid, y'know."

"Never thought you were. Not for a moment."

There was an awkward pause between us. Suddenly, a train thundered past. Both of us jumped, startled. The ground shook underfoot. There was a flash of blurred steel, chrome and glass. A rush of wind pushed against us; followed by a sense of being swept up. Then it was gone. Everything was suddenly quiet and still again and she was smiling at me, the kind of heart-melting smile that Sleeping Beauty must have given Prince Charming when awakened by his kiss.

"Know why I like you?" she purred.

"Uh-uh."

"You don't rag on me 'bout biting my nails or wearing blue lipstick. My folks rag on me all the time. So does my brother, little monster."

"They probably don't mean anything by it."

"You don't know them, or you wouldn't say that. 'Specially my dorky brother. He's a total brat. Can do anything and they never say a word. Just go on spoiling him, thinking it's cute, letting him get away with murder. But I do something, anything, like bite my nails or dye my hair green, they go ballistic. It's not fair. I mean, everyone at the hospital said my hair was totally cool. Even Dr. Lesavoy thought it was awesome and he's a frigging shrink. But not my folks. My dad. Tells my mom I can't come home till my hair's back to normal and I get the earring out of my nose."

"Doesn't that hurt?"

"What?"

"Getting your nose pierced for an earring?"

"I dunno. I was on Ecstasy when I got it done."

I sipped my coffee, not quite sure what to say next. It was the first sip I'd taken and I almost gagged.

"What's wrong? she asked.

"Someone put salt instead of sugar in my coffee."

"I hate it when that happens," she said. If she was mocking me, I couldn't tell. Her gold-flecked amber eyes were bright with innocence as she said: "How come you don't ask me my name?"

"Guess I forgot. What *is* your name?"

"Audra. What's yours?"

"Fish Eggs," I said, but I was smiling.

"I'll call you Shane," she said. "That was the name of my dog. My dad named him, but he was really mine. Big ol' collie-shepherd mix. Used to follow me everywhere, even to school. Then my brat brother came along and Shane forgot all about me and started following him. Don't know why, 'cause Randy was always doing mean stuff to him, like chewing on his ears or pulling his tail. But Shane didn't mind. Never snapped or tried to bite him or anything. Just kept trotting along behind him, like a shadow. Everyone thought it was so cute. 'Specially Mom and Dad. Should've seen 'em. Always taking pictures of them together, you know, just like in that yucky TV commercial—"

"A 'Kodak moment'?"

She nodded, "'Nuff to make you throw up," her gaze following a seagull as it came slanting past overhead. "I kept hoping it would stop. Kept hoping Shane would come back to me or run away or something. But he never did. I knew then it wasn't gonna stop, was gonna go on forever. So... " She paused, smiling as if she knew a secret, then: "But it didn't. The night before I went into hospital, Shane got killed in a fire."

"How?"

"Got trapped in the garage when the door somehow got stuck. Shane slept there at night on an old mattress. A spark from the water-heater caused it, they think. By the time the firemen broke down the door, he'd been burned to death."

"I'm sorry."

She shrugged. "Served him right in a way. He'd still be alive if he hadn't started following my little brother."

"How d'you mean?"

"When he was my dog, he slept on my bed. Mom wouldn't let him do that with Randy. Said Shane might smother him, him being so little and everything. So they shut Randy's door. That's when Shane started howling and they put him in the garage. I told 'em he could sleep on my bed again, but, like always, they wouldn't listen. So you see, it was their fault, not mine." She sipped her coffee, gazing out to sea as she became lost in her thoughts.

A cool breeze came off the ocean. It felt like an icy hand. My sweat prickled and I shivered. "Well, I better hit the shower," I said. "Thanks for the coffee."

She smiled, a frightening little smile that never reached her eyes.

"You can't go yet."

"Why not?"

"I haven't told you why my dad called me Audra."

"Okay. But then I really have to go in."

"He had the biggest crush on Linda Evans in that old TV show, *Big Valley*. That was her name, y'know. Audra."

"Yeah, I remember. It's pretty."

"Y'think? I hate it." She smirked, adding: "He still has, I think. A crush, I mean. Watches reruns all the time on cable. Late at night, you know, after mom's gone to bed." She paused, as if amused by her thoughts, then: "One time I woke up thirsty and came down to get a Coke. He didn't hear me and as I went into the kitchen, know what I saw him doing?"

"I can guess," I said.

"And he calls *me* dysfunctional. I wanted to tell mom, so she'd know what he was doing, and why he wasn't hot for her any more, but Dr. Lesavoy said I shouldn't. Said it wouldn't change anything and would only stir things up and things were already bad enough. So, I didn't. But I still wanted to. Do you have any matches?"

"Sorry. I don't smoke."

"Me, neither. I just love fireflies."

Before I could question the connection, she dug into her jeans and came out with a handful of wooden kitchen matches. "This is all I got left." She struck one on the cement step, gazing fixedly at it as the flame flared, then threw it into the air. It arced, flame sputtering, and went out as it landed on the dew-soaked grass. A second, third and fourth match followed, all dying on the grassy mound.

"Beautiful, aren't they? Don't you just love fireflies? No, don't touch them!" she exclaimed as I went to pick them up. "They're mine. I have to bury them or they won't go to heaven." She picked up the four spent matches, holding them lovingly in her open palm. "One day they're going to teach me how to fly."

I didn't know what to say. I wasn't sure if she was acting this way to keep my attention, or if she were a little crazy. I watched as she walked down the steps and across the path to the edge of the cliff and looked down at the railroad tracks. She spread out her arms, like wings, and for a moment I panicked.

"No, don't!" I shouted. "Audra, wait!" I ran toward her.

She turned and looked at me, arms still outstretched.

"Just like a grown-up," she said mockingly. "You guys take the fun out of everything."

"Sorry. Guess I wasn't thinking straight."

"It's okay, I forgive you." She leaned close and kissed me, her lips icy cold against my flushed cheek. "I have to go now. My dad's driving down with my little brat brother. They've been camping out last few days. Mountains, somewhere. I want to be sure everything's ready for them when they get here. 'Bye."

"G'bye," I said. I watched her run, arms now stretched out like airplane wings, along the path toward the beach. The breeze coming in off the ocean carried her voice back to me.

"'Bye, Shane... 'Bye... " Getting fainter. "'Bye, Shane... 'Bye... 'Bye... " Then her voice, and she, were gone.

I felt a sense of relief. I took a deep breath, filling my lungs with cool tangy ocean air, and expelled it loudly. I felt better then, more relaxed, and went indoors to take a shower.

The next morning it was on the news. Shortly after midnight, the grim-voiced San Diego newscaster announced, a tragedy had taken the lives of three members of the Stanek family. Mr. and Mrs. Stanek, and their six-year-old son were killed in a fire that burned down the Del Mar bungalow they were renting for two weeks. The old wood-frame, shingle-roofed building had somehow burst into flames and within seconds become a fiery inferno, and though firemen responded quickly they weren't able to save anyone trapped inside. The cause of the fire, Captain Avery said, was not known yet. A fourth member of the Stanek family, twelve-year-old Audra, was found wandering around in a daze on the cliffs. When questioned by police about the fire, and why she was not in bed like the rest of her family, Audra—who was recently released from the state mental hospital—said only:

"I was burying fireflies."

St. Christopher and the Little Fisherman

Children sweeten labors, but they make misfortunes more bitter. They increase the cares of life, but they mitigate the remembrance of death.

— Bacon

He sat fishing from the old harbor wall, his dark solemn eyes staring longingly at the deep blue water beyond El Morro. It was as if the waves carried him like a boat out into the Gulf Stream where the real fish were. Real fish. Not the puny things he caught that barely silenced the hunger in his belly, but giants of the sea that only a man dared hunt. The kind of man he would be when he grew up.

But he loved to fish, if only for *roncos*, and he had to eat; so every dawn he got up from his straw mattress, put on the only shirt and pants he owned, collected his fishing line and bait and walked bare-footed from his hovel in the old section of Havana, past the ancient fort, La Punta, and the laurel-shaded Prado, to sit among the beggar children on the *Malecon* wall.

He was a small, skinny, dark-skinned boy, about twelve, who seemed to like everyone; even the half-starved, half-naked beggar children who made fun of the size of the fish he caught and then, when he wasn't looking, tried to steal his catch from the brown paper bag in which he hid them from the sun. But he was too quick for them, always moving the bag out of their reach and waving them away. Watching him as I did each morning from my hotel window across the street, I was puzzled by his tolerance. Most people would have lost their temper with the tenacious little thieves; the boy didn't. He understood their hunger as if it were his own, and seemed more saddened than angered by their attempts to rob him. Once I even saw him share his catch with them. I expected them to be grateful. But hunger outweighs gratitude and the next morning there they were, trying to steal his fish again.

37

I'd watched him for three days now, too busy writing about all I'd seen in my two-week tour of the island to leave the room. But today, tired of being cooped up, I decided to join him. I put on my sunglasses, wheeled myself out of the hotel, waited for the traffic racing along the *Malecon* to slacken, then propelled my chair in his direction. As I approached, he looked up from his fishing, smiled as if pleased to have adult company, and then went on watching his line in the water.

Immediately, beggar children swarmed around me, beseeching me for money. They were so thin and undernourished their ribs stuck out, the ridges between each bone deep enough to hide a man's finger; and in their gaunt, sunken-cheeked faces their dark eyes looked too big for the sockets, giving them the appearance of aliens. I wanted to empty my pockets, to give them every cent I had, but I knew better. Give money to one, and word soon spread and you became a marked man throughout the entire city.

As if sensing my dilemma, the boy spoke sharply to them and the children grudgingly returned to their seats on the low stone wall that ran all along the *Malecon.*

I started to thank the boy, saw he was concentrating on his fishing and fell silent. He sat still, shoulders hunched over, intently watching his line in the water. He held the thin blue line lightly between the forefinger and thumb of each hand, with the end of it tied around a heavy piece of iron that lay at his feet. His body seemed perpetually tensed, coiled almost, ready to jerk the line up at the slightest tug. But no tug came. And presently, he gave an impatient sigh and pulled his line in. He looked even thinner and smaller up close. His shaggy uncut black hair curled down over the soiled collar of his sun-faded salmon-pink shirt, the sleeves of which were worn through at the elbows. The tail of the shirt hung down over old baggy gray pants held up by a twisted horsehair belt that was much too big for him and had to be knotted. The pants were smeared with fish blood, the cuffs frayed around his dirty bare feet. But, impoverished as he was, there was no sign of quit in his eyes and he carried himself with a dignity that refused to accept defeat.

When he'd pulled his line in, he set the cigar-shaped sinker on the wall beside him and carefully examined the hook. A tiny piece of shrimp still clung to it, soggy and useless from its long stay underwater. With another sigh, he pulled the bait loose and threw it into the harbor.

"Bite?" I said.

He smiled, showing me a gap where his top front teeth had been. I pointed at the hook and then at the water, repeating:

"Bite?"

This time he understood. He nodded, held up the hook and with his other hand imitated a fish taking the bait and swimming away. I nodded to show I understood. He smiled again, pleased, for now I was not just another tourist invading his privacy, I was a fellow fisherman and this made us friends.

I watched as he unfolded a piece of soiled newspaper on the wall beside him. The warm tangy wind off the Gulf flapped the paper about, forcing him to hold it down with one knee. Inside, was a small pile of shrimp. He picked one up, expertly pinched off its curled pink tail, peeled away the outer shell, and with the rusty-bladed kitchen knife that hung from his wrist by a leather thong, cut the soft white fleshy meat in half. Putting one half back on the pile, he passed the barbed end of the hook through the other half twice to make sure it didn't come loose when cast into the water. Then, rising, he twirled the hook around his head like a bolas and cast it as far as he could, the lead sinker quickly pulling the line beneath the surface.

"*Un gran pez*," he said, pointing to his line in the water. I nodded, smiling. I spoke very little Spanish but I thought I understood him. To make sure, I held my hands wide apart and said: "*Big fish.*"

"Ah, *si, si.* Mucho beeg feesh."

We both laughed, pleased by our comradeship, then the boy returned his attention to fishing.

Behind us, two of President Batista's soldiers, armed with automatic weapons, walked by. They gave me a suspicious look. I held their gaze for a moment to let them know I was not intimidated nor had anything to hide, then looked away. The soldiers walked on. Fidel Castro and his ragtag rebels were fighting the Cuban Army in the Sierra Maestra Mountains around Santiago, and rebel sympathizers were causing problems in Havana and other major cities. Only last week, on the eve of the Grand Prix of Cuba, sympathizers had kidnapped Formula One Champion, Juan Manuel Fangio (he was later released, unharmed), and, on Sunday, poured oil on the streets, causing the racecars to lose control and crash into the barriers. Officials were forced to stop the race and award it to Stirling Moss, who was leading at the time. But, despite these embarrassing setbacks, Batista was still in control. His soldiers and dreaded secret police were rounding up anyone who even looked suspicious. The suspects were imprisoned in the dungeons in La Punta or El Morro and tortured until they either died or confessed—guilty or not—to acts of treason for which they were then shot.

The United States' government's reaction to all this was typical: while the President publicly denounced the dictator's actions, the CIA simultaneously supplied arms to both Batista and Castro, quietly biding their time until they were certain which of the opposing factions was going to win out. Then, of course, they would fully endorse the victor and claim that all along they had been backing him. Smart politics, if not entirely ethical.

Meanwhile, tourism in Havana was at its highest peak; it were as if everyone in Miami sensed that time was running out for them and that as soon as Castro took over, he'd shut down the casinos and whorehouses and American-owned hotels and put an end to all the exciting nightlife in what was undoubtedly the gaudiest, sexiest, raunchiest and most-fun-anything-goes city in the world.

That was the reason I was there; to write about the changing times, the gambling and political corruption and the revolution, all of which was tearing Cuba apart. I was also there as a guest of the actor George Raft, for whom I'd written a screenplay, and who had invited me to the grand opening of the new Hilton Hotel, located a few blocks on along the *Malecon*. Having never been to Cuba, and knowing it was about to change forever, I jumped at the offer.

My thoughts were suddenly interrupted as the boy stood up and began pulling in his line. I hoped he'd hooked a fish. But his expression told me he hadn't. He drew in his line, sighed glumly, baited the hook and recast. Same result. He recast a third time and then turned to me, speaking in Spanish while pointing out at the Gulf. I understood only a few words, but managed to figure out that he was telling me that out there was where the big fish were and that one day he would be man enough to catch them. I wished I could help him and remembered with irritation all the fishing tackle that, since I'd lost the use of my legs in a car accident, had been gathering dust in my garage. Here was someone who really could have used it.

"Try again," I said, indicating he should recast. "Maybe this time you'll be lucky." He didn't understand. *"Suerte,"* I said, hoping I was using the right word. *"Muy suerte."*

He nodded, his expression suggesting that he didn't believe he was lucky or was going to get lucky. But he recast anyway, waited a few minutes, then slowly began pulling in his line.

"'Nada," he said resignedly.

I nodded. When he'd hauled in most of the line, it suddenly grew taut and the boy swore in Spanish.

"Rocks?" I said. I don't know if he understood me but he nodded and continued trying to pull his line loose. Suddenly, it snapped and when the boy pulled the line in I saw he had no hook or sinker. The boy stared disgustedly at the empty line and then pointed with the knife, still looped around his wrist, at the water some fifty feet away.

"Cangrejos!"

"You mean, rocks?"

He looked at me, puzzled, head cocked to one side. I made a fist, hoping it looked like a rock, and mimed the hook snagging underneath it. "Rocks," I said several times.

Finally, he understood. *"No, senor. Un cangrejo."*

"No comprendo 'cangrejo,'" I said.

He thought a moment, then shaped his hand like a crab, grabbed at an imaginary piece of bait and scuttled under a rock.

"Crabs!" I exclaimed. "A crab took your bait under a rock."

"*Si, senor. Cangrejos.*" He took a tiny plastic bag from his pocket and removed the last hook from inside it.

"What're you going to use for a sinker?" I asked. When I saw he didn't understand, I shaped my forefinger and thumb to look like a sinker and said: "Sinker."

"*Ah, si. Un plomada.*" He shrugged his gaunt shoulders. "*No mas.*" He began tying the hook onto the line.

"*Un momento, amigo.*" I searched my pockets for something to replace the sinker. Nothing but loose change. I remembered my nail clippers sitting on the bedside table in my hotel room and contemplated going back for them. Then it hit me and I knew it would be perfect, not just in size and weight but spiritually too. I reached behind my neck, felt inside my shirt collar and unclasped the half-dollar-sized St. Christopher medallion that hung from a thin silver chain.

"Here." I removed the chain and handed the medallion to him. "Try this."

He frowned, puzzled.

"Sinker," I said, indicating the medallion. "*Un plomada.*"

"*No, senor.*" He shook his head, refusing to take it.

"But I want you to," I insisted. "Might bring you luck. *Suerte. Muy suerte.*"

Still, he hesitated.

"*Un grande pez,*" I said, pushing the medallion into his grimy little hand. "*Muy suerte. Un grande pez.*"

He hesitated for another moment, uncertain, then he nodded, as if convincing himself that it was all right to use the patron saint of travelers for something as menial as fishing—

"*Gracias, senor, gracias.*"

—and began threading the line through the chain loop on the silver medallion. When he was satisfied it was secure, he rose and twirled the line above his head, finally casting it out as far as he could.

As the medallion sank beneath the waves, I silently prayed, asking St. Christopher to bring my young friend good luck. The boy, meanwhile, stretched and began rubbing circulation back into his scarred, thin, cramped legs. Then he sat on the wall again, the line between his fingers, and we waited for a fish to strike.

I dug out a roll of Lifesavers and offered him one.

"*Gracias, senor.*" He grinned his gap-toothed grin. "*Muy bueno.*"

The waves began slap-slapping against the harbor wall. A fishing boat was churning out into the Gulf. It was all white and rigged for sport-fishing and in the bright morning sunlight I could see a large, white-haired, white-bearded sunburned man at the helm. For a moment I thought it was Hemingway, whom I'd had dinner with yesterday at his *finca* on a hilltop outside Havana; a second look told me it wasn't, but the thought of the ailing novelist reminded me that I should get back to my writing.

Just then the captain saw the boy and waved. The boy waved back and sighed, and I sensed he was wishing he was on that boat heading out into the Gulf where the men fished.

"*Amigo?*" I asked.

"*Si,*" the boy said wistfully. For another moment he looked longingly at the boat, then went back to his fishing.

Suddenly, the line twitched in the boy's fingers. He held his breath. Waited. The line twitched again, violently. He gripped the line and used one knee to snag the slack coiled on the wall.

"*Pecar! Pecar!*" he said excitedly. He began playing out his line, never letting any slack form so that the fish could use its weight to jerk itself free of the hook.

"Beeg feesh!" he said to me. "Beeg! Beeg!" At his shouts the beggar children came running up. They crowded around us, yelling encouragement.

Slowly and carefully, never giving the fish any rest, the boy pulled his catch in. It was a struggle and I kept expecting the line to snap. But under his skilful guidance it didn't and I began to think that St. Christopher had stepped in to help.

Someone elbowed their way through the beggar children and joined me at the wall. I saw it was a tall, light-skinned boy of about fourteen who wore well-pressed tan slacks, a bright green shirt, polished black shoes, and looked as arrogant as a matador.

Ignoring me, he spoke rapidly in Spanish to the boy, his tone superior and demanding. The boy on the wall replied without turning his head. I didn't understand what he said but there was no mistaking the alarm in his voice.

"What is it?" I asked. "*Que pasa?*"

The light-skinned boy turned to me and said, calmly and in smugly-perfect English: "Armando is worried his line will break. He knows it was not made for such a big fish."

Slowly, a pile of line grew at Armando's feet as he brought the fish nearer the wall. The strain on the line increased and only the boy's skill and painstaking care saved it from breaking. As I watched the struggle, my gaze fixed on the water around the line, I noticed some rocks showing directly below us. They hadn't been there when I first arrived and I realized the tide must be going out.

Another loud shout of encouragement erupted from the beggar children as a blur of silver, white and pale blue broke surface and threshed wildly against the tautly stretched line.

"Tiburon! Tiburon!"

"Armando has caught himself a shark," the light-skinned boy informed me. "That is too bad, for it does not make good eating."

"Well, you don't have to sound so damned smug about it," I snapped before I could catch myself.

The light-skinned boy looked surprised that anyone had the nerve to address him that way. But before he could reply, there was a big splash below us. A gasp came from the beggar children as the shark, already swimming toward the surface, was swept up by an incoming wave. The added momentum lifted the large fish onto the rocks, where it lay flopping for a few moments, then spun around and splashed back into the water.

Armando said something quickly to the light-skinned boy, glancing at me as he did.

"What's wrong?" I said. "What's he want?" Still irked by the way I'd spoken to him earlier, the light-skinned boy ignored me. I grabbed his arm and jerked him close. "I said, what's he want?"

"Armando says he has to kill the shark quickly or the line will break, and he doesn't know how to do it."

"Why doesn't he just cut the line?"

The light-skinned boy hesitated, debating whether he should bother to tell me the reason, then condescendingly said: "Because the shark has something of yours, senor; something very valuable that Armando says he mustn't lose."

"If he means the medallion," I said, "tell him to forget it. It's not important. I don't mind losing it."

"But that would be very rude of Armando," the light-skinned boy said in a taunting voice. "For it has brought him luck. He has finally proved he is man enough to catch a big fish."

"I don't care what he's proved," I said. "Just do as I say. Tell Armando to cut the damn line."

Shrugging, the light-skinned boy turned to tell Armando what I'd said. But it was too late. Armando had already handed the line to one of the beggar children and now scrambled to the edge of the wall, intending to lower himself onto the rocks below.

"Hey! I yelled, grabbing for his arm. "Come back! Are you nuts? You'll be killed down there!"

If he understood me, he didn't reveal it. He grinned at me and dropped down onto the rocks. I gripped the arms of my wheel-chair and pulled myself to my feet. Unable to stand unsupported, I leaned forward, straddling the sun-baked wall with my body, and yelled for Armando to come back, to get back up here beside me!

He didn't answer. I watched, alarmed, as he kneeled down on the edge of the rocks and shouted over his shoulder at the beggar child holding the line.

"Armando wants Raul to bring the shark closer," the light-skinned boy told me matter-of-factly. "So he can kill it and get back your—"

"Shut up!" I told him. Helpless, I looked down as below on the rocks Armando, knife in hand, waves spraying over him, waited tensely for the shark to surface again.

"Armando!" I yelled at him. "For God's sake don't—"

I stopped as I saw the long, silvery-blue body of the shark swim past the boy, its mouth a gash of teeth as it rolled over on its back. It was now beside the rocks. Armando leaned out over the water and plunged his knife into the shark. The startled fish jerked away, knife still in it, the weight of its body pulling Armando off the rocks and into the water.

I held my breath. Screams came from the beggar children along the wall. The light-skinned boy absently picked his nose, more curious than concerned about the struggle below.

In the water, Armando tried frantically to slip the thong off his wrist. But the leather held and the last I saw of the boy was the blackened, calloused soles of his feet, thrashing in the waves, as he was dragged under by the shark.

✠

The Butterfly Bomb

Your little child is your only true democrat.

– Mrs. Stowe

The two young boys couldn't wait until class was over, ending a tiresome school-day that had been routinely interrupted by air-raids; squadrons of German bombers droning overhead that had driven them, along with their classmates and the rest of the school, scurrying into the big steel and concrete shelter at the rear of the playground. There, huddled together on long narrow benches, backs pressed against the damp concrete wall, knees so close to the boy opposite that the teacher had trouble squeezing by, they continued their lessons; everyone, children and teachers alike, trying not to wince or even acknowledge the bombs falling, but feeling a cold rush of fear as the ground shook and their ears vibrated with each explosion, praying, some silently, some aloud, and at the same time hearing the steady muffled pounding of the anti-aircraft guns that were trying to shoot down the enemy planes. Since early morning, the sirens had wailed incessantly, first the alert, then the all-clear, sometimes coming so close together it was difficult to remember which one they were listening to…

But now it was late afternoon and the drudgery was almost over; four more minutes and the school bell would ring, allowing everyone to escape.

Eric Grantley and the boy seated beside him, Alfie Jackson, kept one eye on the teacher, the other on the wall-clock, as they furtively slipped their homework books into their satchels so they'd be ready to dart out of the classroom the instant the bell sounded. Eric and Alfie were best friends. Closer than brothers and inseparable during daylight hours, they'd managed to compile the biggest shrapnel collection in all of East Sheen, a small suburb of London. The envy of every boy in the neighborhood, they kept these highly-prized chunks of high-explosive bombs, incendiaries, shot-down

German aircraft, and spent machinegun bullets in Eric's dad's tool-shed, in a metal trunk fastened by a large padlock that had taken two weeks' of combined pocket money to buy. Only they had the keys to open it and only they knew where those two keys were hidden. Their parents didn't under-stand the boys' passion, and whenever asked about it they'd shake their heads and say derogatory things like "My God, you'd think they had the Crown Jewels locked in there, way they guard all that junk," and "Well, I don't know about you, but I think it's downright morbid, keeping stuff that killed people!"

Eric and Alfie couldn't care less what anyone thought; it was their collection, and they had the scraped knees, scabby elbows and broken fingernails—caused by months of climbing over and digging under mountains of debris that had once been people's homes—to prove it.

But now the four minutes were up. The bell sounded, ending school. Eric and Alfie, who sat in front where teachers could keep an eye on them, hurried out of class ahead of the other kids and, despite the wall-signs reading POSITIVELY NO RUNNING IN SCHOOL! ran along the hall leading to the front entrance.

⊶▰ ▰⊷

"Where you think we should look, mate?"

"Dunno," Eric said. He was taller than Alfie, but not as broad across the chest and shoulders. His hair was darker, too, and less curly. And he had the look of a choirboy, whereas Alfie looked like a thief on the run. "Sounded like the bombs landed over near Mortlake Bridge."

"That's what I was thinking," Alfie said. "Let's take a gander over there first, eh?"

Mortlake was adjacent to East Sheen, a densely populated low-income area that spread along the banks of the River Thames. Its claim to fame lay in the fact that the famous annual Oxford and Cambridge boat race ended near Mortlake Bridge. Now that the war was on the boat race had been canceled, Parliament and both universities agreeing that the *Luftwaffe* had enough targets to hit without giving them a chance to dive-bomb the huge wildly-cheering crowds that normally lined both banks of the river during the race.

Now, as Eric and Alfie jogged across Mortlake Bridge, they saw black smoke curling up from behind a row of nearby houses.

"C'mon, mate," Alfie said, breaking into a run. "We'd better 'urry, 'fore all the other shrapnel 'unters find the good stuff."

Running hard, Eric and Alfie ducked between the railway-crossing gates that were closing for an oncoming passenger train, and rounded the first corner they came to. Ahead, one whole side of the narrow street had been bombed to the ground. The houses opposite were still standing but every window had been blown out. Broken glass lay everywhere. The bombing had taken place hours ago, and firemen had already put out all the fires. But smoke still drifted up from the rubble and the chilly damp air reeked of burned timbers and wet ashes. People stood in little groups, talking and pointing at the row of demolished homes. Others helped their neighbors try to dig out whatever they could salvage from the smoking debris; while a few just stood there, still in shock over losing everything they possessed.

Eric and Alfie, their emotions calloused by months of death and bombing, darted past the suffering victims and began combing the rubble. Their well-trained eyes searched for any piece of jagged metal that might have come from the exploding bombs. They had gathered a half-dozen pieces worth keeping, when a policeman gestured to them from the pavement and ordered them to leave.

"What for?" Eric demanded. "We ain't stealing nothing."

"Now then, nipper," the Bobby said sternly but without anger, "don't give me no lip. Just do like I say and be on your way. 'Urry up, now, like good lads."

Eric and Alfie scrambled down off the rubble, grumbling all the way.

"Ain't fair is what it is," Alfie said as he and Eric left the street. "'Ow can a bloke find shrapnel if he can't dig around for it, is what I'd like to know."

"Beats me," Eric said. He added darkly: "Seems to me, the police ought to have something better to do than chase us around all day."

"Tell you what," Alfie said. "I 'eard Tommy Jenkins telling someone in class this morning that a bunch of 'ouses up near Sheen Common got bombed last night. Wanna try'n find some stuff up there?"

Satchels flopping against their backs, the two ten-year-olds jogged nonstop up Sheen Lane Road, then uphill another mile or so to the common. A light rain was falling by the time they reached the white-painted entrance gate. The boys ignored it. Turning left, they entered an unpaved tree-lined road running parallel to the ivy-covered common wall. Halfway along it, they found the bombed-out houses. There were five of them, cottages actually, with neat little gardens surrounding each dwelling. Only the middle cottage was totally demolished while the others flanking it had lost their adjacent walls, parts of their roofs and most of their windows. Eric and Alfie, experts in assessing the number of bombs it took to cause different degrees of damage, judged this to be the work of a single bomb, a stray one probably that made a direct hit on the center cottage.

Mulberry Lane, as the road was called, was empty save for a parked car with a cracked windshield and an old white-bearded balding man trimming the hedge around the front garden of the bombed-out cottage. To the casual passerby, it probably seemed like a strange thing to be doing under the circumstances. But the elderly couple who'd been killed in the bombing had been his neighbors and friends for over fifty years. And though he could not bring them back to life, this was his effort to bring some semblance of normalcy to the insanity going on around him, and he wasn't about to be annoyed any further by two young boys.

"Bugger off!" he yelled, waving his shears at them. "You ain't out of my sight by the time I count to three, I'll set the police on you!"

Eric and Alfie poked their tongues out at the old man. But when he opened the gate and came toward them holding his shears, they turned and fled into the sanctuary of the common.

"Seems the 'ole world's against us findin' any shrapnel," Alfie grumbled as they sat on a bench facing the unused public tennis courts. "I mean, what's wrong with everybody, I'd like to know?"

Eric wasn't listening. He'd spotted a yellow canister hanging from the rusted wire fence surrounding the courts.

"You see what I see?" he said, pointing.

Alfie looked, his eyes growing wide with excitement.

"Blimey," he said. "That's a bleedin' butterfly bomb, ain't it?"

Both boys got up and cautiously approached the fence. Once they were close, they could see that one blade of the bomb's little propeller was snagged in the rusty wire.

"Never seen one up this close before," Alfie said.

"Me, neither," said Eric. "Never even seen one that wasn't exploded. Just that tiny orange-colored piece Dave Orvis showed us, remember—day we were over his house?"

Alfie nodded, remembering, but keeping his gaze fixed on the butterfly bomb. The canister, about the size of a large can of baked beans, was painted bright yellow and had red spots on it. Dropped by the *Luftwaffe* in large numbers, the bombs drifted down on their propellers, arming themselves the moment they landed. They were not powerful enough to do much damage to property, but were dropped solely for the purpose of injuring curious children.

"I bet this'll make our collection the biggest in all of London," Alfie said breathlessly. "All of England, prob'ly."

"Yeah, if we could keep it," Eric agreed.

"What d'you mean 'if'? 'Course we're gonna keep it. Finders keepers, right?"

"But we can't," Eric said. "They're supposed to explode the moment you touch 'em. And even if somehow it didn't—doesn't—our parents wouldn't let us keep it. They'd phone the police and then we'd really be in trouble for not calling 'em in the first place, like all the posters tell you to."

Alfie dragged his gaze from the butterfly bomb and looked at Eric as if he were a traitor.

"I don't care what the posters say, or the bleedin' coppers. We found this bomb and I'm keepin' it, so there."

"No, don't," Eric said as Alfie edged closer to the butterfly bomb. "Wait, Alfie." He caught his friend's sleeve and pulled him back.

"Leggo! I'm warnin' you," Alfie said, cocking his fist. "I'll bash you in the nose, if you don't."

"You an' whose army?"

For a long tense moment the two friends stood glaring at each other, fists cocked, ready to fight. Then Alfie lowered his fists and grinned.

"Okay, you win," he said. "Let's go tell someone what we found."

Together, they walked across the common to the gate. There, Alfie stopped, "'Ang on, mate, I got somethin' in me shoe," sat down and started taking off his right shoe.

"We could tell that old man," Eric said, pointing at the white-haired man still trimming his hedge. "He'd probably ring the police for us."

"Maybe," said Alfie. "But I wouldn't get too close to him, if I was you. He might try'n cut you with them shears."

Then, as Eric nodded, not moving:

"Go ahead, mate, while I get rid of this stone in my shoe."

Eric started toward the white-haired man. But, as if not fully trusting his friend, he stopped after a few steps and looked back. Alfie had his shoe off and was feeling inside it for the stone. Satisfied, Eric continued on.

But when he was a short distance from the white-bearded man, who had stopped clipping and was now glaring at him, Eric looked back again and saw Alfie was gone. His heart jumped. Whirling around, he ran back to the common. There, at the gate, he saw his friend running across the grass toward the butterfly bomb. He had a fifty-yard start, and even though Eric sprinted as hard as he could, he knew he'd never catch Alfie.

Ahead, Alfie now reached the tennis courts and cautiously reached up to the butterfly bomb.

Eric, even as he yelled for Alfie not to touch it, saw the flash and heard the roar as the bomb exploded.

It was a sound and a sight he remembered for the rest of his life.

☩

Jeunesse

*Call not that man wretched, who, whatever ills he suffers, has
a child to love.*

– Southey

Joe Max loved children. Though a confirmed bachelor who had no kids
of his own (strangely, he didn't want any), he possessed a love for children that bordered on the abnormal. Quiet and withdrawn among
adults, shy with women, he opened up like a flower in the sun when he
was around kids. And not just kids he knew. Strangers. Children he'd never
met before. Introverted children, angry children, delinquents who'd been
kicked out of foster homes, it didn't matter who they were or what they'd
done—Joe Max loved them and they all responded to him as if he were
their favorite uncle.

I'm sure by now you've already visualized what Joe Max looked like.
Santa Claus probably came to mind. Or maybe a big warm cuddly bear of a
man with a smile that could light up a dark room. Or any of those wonderful old men—barbers, milkmen, ice cream vendors—with merry blue eyes
and lovable crinkly smiles that Norman Rockwell depicted on the covers of
Saturday Evening Post.

Well, you couldn't be more wrong. Joe Max was a small, wiry man who
by forty, when this story took place, had thinning sandy brown hair, squinty
gray eyes, and a prematurely-lined, pushed-in face that could have passed for
the bottom of an old bucket. I'm not kidding. On top of that, his voice was
raspy and his uneven teeth were stained brown by incessant cups of black
coffee and an occasional wad of chewing tobacco.

But none of this mattered. Not to children. Unlike adults, they saw past
Joe's ugly, gnomish appearance and looked within him, into his heart; and
there they found the only thing they cared about or needed: his love.

Joe, in turn, apparently found what he needed in them: *their* love. Which is why what happened to him in Africa had such an adverse affect on him and came as close to destroying him as anything ever could.

I first met Joe Max in the little basement laundry room of our Sherman Oaks' apartment building. I'd just given up acting and was trying to become a serious writer. As I stood there by the drier, folding my still-warm underwear, Joe entered with a basket of dirty clothes. We got to talking. He said he'd just come back from Cuba, where he'd fought alongside Fidel Castro in the revolution. Nowadays that would brand him as a communist; but in 1959, you have to remember, Castro was considered by most Americans to be a rebel with a cause; a patriot fighting to rid his country of its ruthless dictator, President Batista.

I'd never met a mercenary—or idealist, as Joe Max called himself—and I was fascinated by the idea of someone voluntarily risking his neck for strangers. Joe brushed over the subject casually, saying that he'd fought in Korea to save the South Koreans from being oppressed by the communists, so why not do the same for the Cuban people, who were more or less our neighbors. Simple as that.

I saw Joe Max a few times after that, generally as he was coming and going from his apartment, and once when he was playing Santa Claus at the Broadway Department store. He was sitting on a chair in the traditional plumped-up Santa Claus outfit, wearing a red stocking cap and a fake white beard, and there were kids climbing all over him. Joe was beaming and talking to them in a fake, deep Santa Claus voice and as I watched him, I realized I'd never seen a happier human being. Shortly after that, I moved out of the apartment building and didn't see or hear from him for about two years.

By then I'd moved from the Valley to Brentwood, into a one-bedroom cubbyhole overlooking the Veteran's Hospital, a sprawling complex of buildings and landscaped grounds on the corner of Wilshire and San Vicente Boulevards. One morning as I was walking to the local bagel shop, I saw a man in old faded military fatigues standing on the lawn staring out through the fence that surrounded the property. It was Joe Max. He looked much older and sadder and I didn't recognize him at first, but after a second look I realized who it was and hurried over to him.

If he saw me coming, he didn't acknowledge it. Nor did he answer when I spoke to him through the metal bars of the fence. He continued to stare off into space, expressionless, no sign of recognition in his squinty, red-rimmed eyes.

"Joe," I said, puzzled. "It's me, Simon. You know, from the Del Vista Apartments in Sherman Oaks? You lived below me, remember?"

He didn't respond. Didn't even look at me. He just turned and walked slowly across the large green lawn, through the trees and across the road, into one of the buildings.

I guess I should have let it end there. But I couldn't. In the short time I'd known Joe I'd grown to like him. And though we weren't what you'd call buddies, I was concerned enough about his strange behavior to try to find out what had caused it.

I went to the administration building and explained what had happened to the receptionist at the front desk. She wasn't very helpful, but I finally persuaded her to let me talk the psychiatrist she said was handling Joe's case.

Dr. Bernard Korngold was a large, overweight man in his early forties who wore a rumpled dark suit, peered at me through the thick lenses of his rimless glasses, and had a comb-over that looked like a black squid squashed on top of his bald head. But he was gentle-voiced, compassionate, and genuinely interested in what I had to say about Joe Max.

"No big surprise," he said when I'd finished my story. "Mr. Max has hardly spoken to anyone since he was admitted three months ago."

"How'd you know who he was or why he needed help, then?"

"Had it all written down, neat and precise as a term paper. It even described to us why he needed help."

"He knows what's wrong with him?"

"According to him, yes. Of course, I don't necessarily agree with his diagnosis. But with time and therapy, I'm sure we'll be able to find out what's at the core of Joe's problem."

"Can you tell me what he thinks it is?"

"No," Dr. Korngold said. "That's confidential—between Joe and the medical staff."

"Can't you even give me a clue? I mean, does he think he's schizoid or paranoid or that he hates his mother, what? I'm only kidding about that last crack," I added, as Dr. Korngold smiled. "No offense, okay?"

"None taken." He looked at the Mickey Mouse watch on his bulky, dark-haired wrist. "I have a patient due here any minute, so I'm afraid we're going to have to break this off. I will tell you this, though," Dr. Korngold added, seeing my disappointment. "From the few sessions I've had with him so far, his main trouble stems from something that happened to him in the Belgian Congo; something to do with children."

"Thanks, doc. Oh, and one last question: is it okay if I come and see Joe occasionally?"

"Absolutely. He's not dangerous. And I'm sure, in his own peculiar way, he'd enjoy seeing you."

I left.

⇢▖▌◉ ◉▐▖⇠

I came to see Joe Max at the Veteran's Hospital twice a week for the next month. For the first two weeks he didn't acknowledge me, merely sitting by the window of his cell-like room, staring out at the grounds in absolute silence. It made conversation difficult, but I managed to find things to talk about, often by reading aloud from the newspaper, all the time hoping that Joe would at least acknowledge my presence, if not talk to me. But he didn't. At the end of two weeks I went and saw Dr. Korngold and asked him if he thought I was harming Joe in any way, or causing him undue stress. He said he didn't think so, but to keep a record of my visits so that even the slightest reaction from Joe could be analyzed and, if important, be included in both the evaluation report and the psycho-logical profile Dr. Korngold was working up on him.

Monday and Wednesday of the third week continued in the same vein; I'd talk and Joe Max would sit, back to me, staring blankly out the window. No response, no reaction, nothing. Frustrated as hell, I left the hospital vowing not to come back. I'd had enough of Joe's silent treatment. I mean, he wasn't a member of my family that I felt obligated to help; hell, Joe wasn't even a close friend. So, why should I waste two mornings a week, every week, trying to communicate with an acquaintance who either didn't want me around or was so deeply immersed in a cataleptic state that he wasn't aware of me or anything else about him?

So, the following Monday I stayed home and washed my car. Or I should say, *started* to wash it. Because shortly after ten, which was the time I always arrived at Joe's room, my phone rang. It was Dr. Korngold. He sounded excited.

"Where the hell are you?" he demanded.

"Home, where d'you think?"

"I meant, why aren't you here—with Joe?"

"What's the point?" I said. "Sonofagun doesn't know I'm there—or doesn't care—so why bother?"

"Because," Dr. Korngold said, and I could picture him grinning his tight-lipped, double-chinned almost ear-to-ear grin, "Mr. Joseph Max just asked me where you were."

"Be right over!" I said, once I'd recovered from the shock.

⇒─▶◉ ◉◄─⇐

"Why," I asked Joe Max, when we were sitting across the small card table in his room, "did you wait so goddamn long to talk?"

He looked at me, head cocked slightly to one side, and with a perfectly straight face, said: "Why should I talk when you were doing enough for both of us?"

I swear to God, that's exactly what he said. I wanted to hit him.

"You moron," I said. "You stupid dumb sonofabitch. D'you realize how worried everyone around here's been about you?"

He shrugged, "That's what they get paid for," and looked calmly out the window. A gardener was cutting the lawns with a power mower. I waited until the whining roar of the mower had passed, then said angrily:

"Well, maybe they do, but I don't, and if you think I've got nothing better to do than come here twice a week just so's I can read the goddamn newspaper to you—well, you got another think coming!"

Joe studied me, squinty-eyed, as if trying to figure me out.

"Why *do* you come?" he asked quietly.

I started to give him a snappy answer; then realized it was an honest question that deserved and honest answer. I mulled it over a moment before finally saying:

"Ever read John Donne?"

"'No Man Is An Island'?"

"Nobody's said it better."

Again, Joe Max studied me, only this time I saw respect in his squinty blue eyes.

"You really care that much about me?"

"Up until about five minutes ago, when I found out you'd been stringing me along, yeah."

That seemed to cut into him. He said evenly:

"I wasn't stringing you along. I'd taken a vow of silence."

"Since when?"

"Since I left Katanga."

"Katanga? Thought you were in the Congo?"

"Katanga's in the Congo. It's a new, independent state, formed in 1960 or '61 by its president, Moise Tshombe."

"Oh," I said. Then, regaining my train of thought: "Mind if I ask why? You left, I mean?"

"Jeunesse."

"Jer-ness?"

"It's what the Belgians and the mercs call the young hard core Baluba rebel movement. Means, literally, The Youth. The Baluba chiefs recruit them from the tribe, get 'em all hopped up on drugs and then turn 'em loose." Joe paused, his ugly pushed-in face reflecting the pain he felt from his memories.

"Look," I said, "you don't have to tell me this if you don't want to."

Joe Max waited for the power mower to pass by his window; then, as if I hadn't spoken, said quietly:

"I have to tell someone. Keeping it all pent up inside is eating me alive."

I waited. The gardener with the power mower came and went past the window again, then headed off in the direction of the next huge lawn. As the angry whirring noise faded, Joe said:

"They're kids mostly, ten to sixteen on average, some even as young as seven or eight. And you know how I love kids. But after fighting against them, seeing them in action, I realized the *Jeunesse* aren't kids; they aren't even human. They're the devil incarnate."

"Why? What do they do?"

Joe squeezed his brow together, as if trying to squeeze away a migraine.

"I've seen a lot of torturing done in my life. I'm not proud of the fact, but I guess in my profession it's to be expected. But never, ever did I think I'd see a human being doing to another human being what these kids did to anyone they captured."

"Charming."

"They start by cutting their prisoners' arms off at the elbow, their legs off at the knee, then they shove pointed bamboo stakes up their anus and stick the stakes in the ground, dancing and whooping it up while the poor bastard's screaming his head off, begging to be killed. Then, while he's still alive, they cut off his genitals and dance around waving them on sticks. They then cut open his belly and eat his intestines… the victim sometimes still conscious enough to know what's going on… until the witch doctor comes along and cuts out the victim's heart and holds it up for all to see, the heart still beating in his hands." He paused, agonizing over his thoughts, before adding: "Finally, they douse the corpse with gasoline, set it on fire and eat the cooked flesh like it was goddamn steak or prime rib."

He stopped and didn't continue.

I didn't know what to say. He was right. How could this kind of atrocity be going on today, at a time when man was supposed to be civilized? And these were just kids.

As if reading my mind, Joe said: "And these are just kids. *Kids*, Simon. The things I love most in the entire world. In fact, the only thing I ever loved or cared about. And I had to kill them or let them kill me. Kids! I gunned down kids! More than I could count. Watched 'em die. And you know what? When they're dead, these little monsters look just like any other child. I know, 'cause I had to look into their faces, their eyes. Eyes that burned their way into my brain. Day and night I saw them. Even when I tried to sleep, there they were. Always watching me… blaming me for murdering them—" He broke off, distraught, and remained silent for several minutes. Then, in a tortured voice I barely recognized, he said: "I still see them, Simon. Every time I close my eyes and try to go to sleep, there they are, staring at me, cursing me, haunting my very soul. And because of that, goddammit, I can't bring myself to talk to kids anymore. Any kids."

"Why not?"

He didn't answer; didn't look at me.

"Surely you're not comparing them to the kids here," I said, guessing that this was exactly what he was doing. "Christ, we may have an occasional bad seed—maybe more than we should—but the average American kid doesn't barbeque his neighbor and eat his liver just because they don't get along."

I could tell Joe Max wasn't listening. He stared out the window at the blackbirds now greedily gobbling up bugs and worms from the new-mown grass.

"I don't want to talk anymore," he said, without turning from the window. "That okay with you?"

"Sure." I stood up. "Would you like me to drop by tomorrow or Wednesday?"

He moved his head in a way that could have meant anything. I went to the door, "See you, Joe," and walked out.

When I got back to my apartment, I called Dr. Korngold. But he was with a patient, and had other patients lined up all day.

"Don't bother to say I called," I told the operator. "I'll see him tomorrow when I stop by the hospital."

But the next day I was writing too well to stop and it was Wednesday before I got over to see him. He was sitting behind his desk, chewing on his nails.

"That's a hell of a thing for a shrink to do," I kidded him.

He rolled his eyes. "You don't think we have problems, too?" Before I could answer, he added: "He's gone, you know."

"Joe?"

Dr. Korngold nodded his head and rubbed his hand flatly over the few black hairs plastered down on top of his bald head. It looked so much like he was wearing a squashed squid, I wondered if anyone had ever told him about it.

"Checked himself out last night. No explanation, no forwarding address, no nothing. Just up and disappeared. Not that that isn't his legal right, you understand. It is. He entered here on his own volition and he left the same way."

I was surprised, but not that surprised. I shrugged.

"Probably just needed some time off to think."

"Do you know something I don't?" he asked sus-piciously.

"Like, what?"

"Like, what you guys talked about on Monday."

"Wasn't anything special," I said, adding: "I'm sure Joe will tell you about it when he wants to."

And that's how I left it. I never heard from Dr. Korngold again. Or Joe Max. But I did see him occasionally. It was always in the little green park that ran along the cliff-tops on Ocean Avenue in Santa Monica. Homeless men and women frequented the park, gathering in little groups during the day, sleeping under newspapers or in cartons at night. Joe was one of them. It took a moment to recognize him, because he had a beard and was wearing a World War Two steel helmet, aviator glasses, camo fatigues, and boots—and propelling himself along on an old skateboard that he rode like a scooter. I don't think he saw me and I didn't speak to him. What was the point? Neither of us would have known what to say if we had met. I know I wouldn't have.

I mean, what do you say to a man who thinks he's lost everything precious to him?

Humpty Dumpty Had a Great Fall

Childhood has no forebodings; but then it is soothed by no memories of outlived sorrow.

– George Eliot

One afternoon, just before Christmas, ten-year-old Eric Grantley and his mother walked to the corner of Upper Richmond Road and caught the bus to London. Eric's older sister, Elaine, was starring in *Humpty Dumpty*, a pantomime playing at the Prince of Wales Theater. Eric didn't want to go. He and Elaine didn't get along and the last thing he wanted to do was waste one of his precious days during the Christmas Holidays watching a bunch of stupid dancers and singers all made up to look like eggs. But his mother had insisted and when she insisted he do something, which wasn't often, Eric had learned it was best to obey her. So, he'd put on a clean white shirt, his blue school blazer and tie, polished his shoes and accompanied his mother to the bus stop.

Halfway there the air-raid siren sounded. The drone of approaching enemy aircraft followed almost immediately, forcing them to duck into the public shelter on Elm Road. There in the dank-smelling half-light they waited, listening as German bombers roared overhead. Ack-ack guns pounded away at them. But East Sheen wasn't today's target and no bombs fell. The roar of the planes faded. Shortly, the all-clear sounded and the Grantleys left the shelter. Outside, it had started raining, adding to Eric's misery, and he complained bitterly when his mother told him to open his umbrella.

"But I've got my raincoat on."

"I know, dear."

"Then why do I have to use my umbrella?"

"To keep your head dry, dear."

"But I've got me cap for that."

"'My' cap, dear. Please try to speak correctly."

"What's the difference? Me or my? You know what I'm talking about, don't you?"

"Of course, dear. It's just that gentlemen don't say me."

"I don't wanna be a gentlemen. Gentlemen are snobs and I hate snobs."

Mrs. Grantley sighed. She was an extremely gentle, patient woman who never complained and who always found good in everyone. Which, for Eric's sake, was a Godsend, because he could try the patience of Job.

"Eric," she said patiently, "let's not go into that again. Just because circumstances beyond our control—"

"You mean, Dad's stroke—"

"—have forced us to move from our lovely home in Kensington to here, in East Sheen, doesn't make you any less of a gentlemen. Always remember that."

"How can I forget with you'n everyone else in the family always reminding me?"

"One day you'll thank us for it, believe me."

"Bet I won't. Bet I'll never thank you."

"Be that as it may, dearest, please put up your umbrella. I think it's raining harder and you don't want to sit on the bus in a wet raincoat all the way to Piccadilly, do you?"

No, he didn't. But that wasn't the point. The point was:

"Only sissies carry umbrellas," he grumbled.

"Eric, I'm not going to argue with you. Just do as I say and put your umbrella up, there's a good boy."

Eric grudgingly obeyed, praying as he did that none of his neighborhood pals happened to see him walking like a sissy with an umbrella.

By the time they reached Piccadilly Circus, got off the bus and walked to the theater, it was pouring and even Eric was glad he had an umbrella. Elaine had left matinee tickets for them at the box office. The seats were four rows back from the orchestra pit and right on the middle aisle.

"Aren't they lovely seats, dear?" Mrs. Grantley said as they settled into them. "How thoughtful of Elaine to get them for us."

Eric thought they were good seats too, but he wasn't about to admit to it. "'S'only way she can get people to come'n watch her dance," he said, "by buying 'em tickets."

"Your sister's a very fine dancer," his mother said sternly. "You should be awfully proud of her. Now, please be quiet and let me read the program."

The pantomime was wonderfully staged and everyone performing in it was excellent—including Elaine. Even Eric had to admit, albeit grudgingly, that his sister had shined in the spotlight.

Afterward, Eric and his mother went backstage to Elaine's dressing room. It was full of flowers and people congratulating Elaine on her performance. When they'd left, Elaine closed the door and gave her mother a hug.

"Did you enjoy it, darling?"

"Oh, absolutely. It was marvelous, dear. Simply marvelous, and so were you."

"And what did you think of it?" Elaine asked Eric.

"Wasn't bad," he said. "Was jolly good, in fact. 'Specially the way the egg cracked when Humpty Dumpty fell off the wall."

"I thought you'd like that." Elaine winked at her mother, adding: "Well, that clinches it. If my worst critic thinks it was jolly good, how can the rest of London not consider it a complete smash?"

After they left Elaine, mother and son had tea in a little teashop not far from the theater. Rationing had done away with all the fancy cakes and pastries, but the tea was strong and hot and Eric and his mother felt fortified as they left the shop and headed for the bus stop. The rain had stopped, but there was a chilling wind, and being winter it had grown dark. And though it was only a week until Christmas, London was a grim, gloomy place. The blackout hid any lights in the stores, bombed-out buildings were everywhere and the normal Yuletide spirit was missing. In its place, the pain of war reflected in the faces of the people crowding the streets, all anxiously hurrying to get home before the nightly air-raids started.

But tonight it wasn't to be. As Eric and his mother made their way across Piccadilly Circus to the bus stop, the sirens sounded. Normally there was a few minutes' wait before the planes arrived, but for the second time that day the drone of approaching enemy aircraft came almost on top of the sirens. Moments later ack-ack guns in Hyde Park opened up. Flashes lit up the dark sullen sky, illuminating the network of barrage balloons protecting the city. Searchlights striped the clouds, pinpointing enemy bombers. More gunfire; more flashes. Bombs began falling, their high-pitched whistling descent adding to the crowd's terror.

Eric and his mother were swept up by the panicked crowd, as everyone raced for the nearest entrance to the Underground. The train tracks were in tunnels deep below the ground, making them an ideal refuge from the bombs. Nightly, thousands of Londoners slept on the tracks after the trains stopped running and the electricity was turned off.

Now, though, the trains were running and the mob of normal workers descending the steps was tripled by the sudden onslaught of people fleeing from the bombs. Eric and his mother were caught up in the middle of the pack, crushed on all sides, their feet barely touching the steep flight of steps.

"Grab my hand!" Mrs. Grantley screamed at her son; then as she realized it was impossible: "The rail, Eric! Hold onto the rail!"

Eric, separated from his mother by a wedge of panicked men and women, clung to the center handrail and tried not to miss a step as the crowd surged downward. Cries of, "Stop pushing! Stop pushing!" came from the people in front.

Their shouting was drowned out by the deafening roar of a bomb exploding opposite the entrance to the Underground. A tall building collapsed in flames. The blast hurled debris everywhere. Some of it smashed into the crowd, jamming the entrance. Many were injured and the rest, survival their only thought, hurled themselves down the steps. The sudden added weight of all their bodies was too much for the people crammed below. As one they stumbled forward, many losing their balance, held up only by the crowd around them.

Then, a woman near the bottom missed her step. She went down, screaming, dragging and tripping others along with her. Nor did it stop there. The people directly behind her, unable to stop, fell also. And as they fell, they brought others down with them. They, in turn, caused others to fall. And so on. It soon became a human snowball. More and more people kept falling... until those trapped at the bottom of the pile were being crushed to death by the sheer weight of human bodies.

Eric felt his hand torn from the handrail. He was carried downward by everyone packed about him. Screams and shouts filled his ears. A woman's fist accidently hit him in the mouth. As he cried out, some-one's knee buried into his stomach, cutting off his breath. Frantic, he looked around for his mother. She was hidden from him by the sea of heads bobbing in front of him. He prayed that she wasn't hurt. Then more bombs exploded outside near the Underground entrance, adding to every-one's panic.

A man's flailing elbow struck Eric between the eyes, stunning him. He went down, dazed, and instantly felt himself being trodden on by people fighting to get down the steps. Barely conscious, he was swept downward, first on his back, now on his side, twisting, almost suffocated by the mass of entangled bodies who kicked, punched and elbowed him from all angles, their shouts and screams seeming to come from a long way off.

Then it was over. The falling finally stopped. Eric, still dazed, pushed someone lying on top of him aside and sat up. He was near the bottom of the steps. He couldn't see his mother anywhere. He looked back up the steps. They were covered with injured, crawling, moaning bodies. He looked below him. It was worse. People were not only injured, many were not moving at all and Eric, all too-familiar with death, knew they were dead.

Then he saw his mother. She was to his left, crawling over people toward him. Her new blue hat was gone, her hair was a mess, cheeks scratched and bleeding, and one sleeve of her brown raincoat was torn off. Otherwise, she was alive and basically unhurt.

Eric felt a great wave of relief flooding through him. He jumped up, pushing and elbowing everyone aside to get to her.

"Oh, mum," he said, hugging her, "I thought you were dead."

"Not me," Mrs. Grantley said, stroking his head. "You know I'd never leave you." She blinked away tears and kissed the top of his head. "How about you, dearest? Are you all right?"

"I'm fine," Eric said. "My head hurts where somebody punched it and my knee's bleeding, but that's all."

"Splendid," his mother said. "Thank God for small mercies." She gave him another kiss and then stepped back and surveyed the chaos about them. "Now, why don't we try to see if we can help some of these poor people who weren't as fortunate as we were?"

Three Caballeros

What is childhood but a series of happy delusions?

– Sydney Smith

When I was a boy growing up in England, the only person I ever wanted to be was Errol Flynn. Now maybe (as my father constantly reminded me) that wasn't aiming my sights too high, but as far as movie stars living in that era—the 30s and 40s—Flynn was as glamorous and famous as any star around.

And I wanted to be a movie star.

Not an actor, you understand, that was too mundane. A movie star! And when anyone asked me how I could be one without the other, I answered that I was going to be discovered by a studio talent scout, who would test me, give me a starring role and, fast as that (I'd snap my fingers), I'd be an overnight success. After all, I added, according to the movie magazines it happened all the time.

So much for childish naiveté. No one took me seriously, of course—after all, most kids in those much-simpler days saw themselves as Captain Blood or Robin Hood or General Custer, so one more daydreamer didn't exactly cause any waves. Especially since no one in my family or circle of friends believed I'd ever *go* to Holly-wood, let alone become a movie star. But I believed it. I believed it with all my heart. And I became belligerent when anyone tried to suggest otherwise.

It was my fate, I insisted. My destiny. All I had to do, I believed, was wait for precisely the right moment, then whoever controls such things would lean down and tap me on the shoulder and that would be it. Instant movie star. Instant Errol Flynn.

So I waited. And waited. And…

But nothing happened that even vaguely suggested my time was coming. On the contrary, once Hitler invaded Poland and the war started, followed by the incessant bombing of London, I began for the first time to doubt my place in cinematic history. I mean, the way things looked, I'd be lucky if I even stayed alive.

But Fate, like God, moves in mysterious ways. And what seemed to be an ominous ending to a wonderful childhood dream, eventually proved to be the "tap on the shoulder" I'd been waiting for.

It went like this: One Saturday afternoon in 1944, shortly before the Allies invaded Normandy, I was walking alongside the Thames in Richmond, a charming river resort on the outskirts of London. I was thirteen and on my way to go skating, when three American GI's asked me for directions to the ice rink. I told them I was going there and if they wanted, they could come with me. They did, introducing themselves as Hank, Buzz and Gary from the US of A. As we walked I asked them a lot of questions about America, especially Hollywood, which seemed to amuse them. But they answered every one of them, gave me chewing gum, and when we got to the rink insisted on paying my way in. Inside, we skated around together and I introduced them to some of the older girls I knew. That's when I found out they called themselves The Three Caballeros (after characters in a Disney cartoon). They were great guys, fun-loving and full of hell, and they treated the war as if it were one big party they'd been invited to by Uncle Sam. In fact, their biggest worry was, now that America had joined the Allies, the war might not last long enough for them to get into the pants of all the dames they planned to sweep off their feet. My spirits soared. If my heroes, the Yanks, believed the war was almost over, who was I to argue? Admittedly, Hank, Buzz and Gary weren't exactly grizzled veterans. But all three were eighteen, the age when boys become men, and that was good enough for me.

I was tall for my age and looked older, and when I told the Three Caballeros how much I wanted to go to America and become a movie star, they didn't laugh or ridicule me, or even try to discourage me. In fact Buzz, who said he lived at Malibu Beach, next door to Clark Gable and Rita Hayworth, told me to look him up if I ever made it to the States. Hell, he'd introduce me to lots of movie stars! Unable to believe my luck, I tried to return the favor by offering to show them around Richmond any time they wanted. The girls offered to do the same thing and the way they said it, I knew they were offering a lot more than a guided tour. So I wasn't surprised when Hank turned me down. Then he gave me a big wink and whispered that if I was looking for kicks I should come up to Piccadilly Circus tomorrow, where they hung around on weekends picking up dames. I said I would and that night I couldn't go to sleep I was so excited about my upcoming ad-venture.

Sunday, a double-decker let me off near the roundabout and sure enough, there was Buzz talking to two girls outside a Black & White milk bar. He saw me get off the bus, quickly excused himself from the girls, and pulled me into a doorway. Here, he explained that Gary and Hank were on dates and he needed me to take one of the dames off his hands. Her name was Cora. She was about nineteen, styled her long blonde hair peek-a-boo fashion like Veronica Lake, and, according to Buzz, was dying to spread her legs. But I'm only thirteen, I said. Shoot, he said. Just my damn luck. Then he said: Know what? Cora'll never know less you tell her. And anyway, all I need is to get the two dames separated. What happens after that 'tween you'n Cora don't mean diddly squat to me. When I hesitated, doubtful, he said: Don't you want to live with me at Malibu when you make it across the Big Pond? Meet all my movie star buddies?

Naturally, I went like a choirboy led to the altar.

And that, without my knowing, was Fate's tap on my shoulder. Because even though Cora never believed I was Buzz's Limey cousin or that I was nineteen, she went with me anyway because she knew that was what her girlfriend wanted. And that scored big with Buzz; and with Hank and Gary when Buzz later explained how I'd helped him out. Now I was really their buddy.

For the next six weeks I spent every Saturday and Sunday with the Three Caballeros. I don't know why they wanted a 13-year-old boy hanging around with them (my older brothers and sisters certainly didn't), but they did. What's more, they knew I didn't have much money, so they paid for everything. Somehow they even got me a U.S. Army private's uniform and Buzz gave me a GI haircut, so the girls they picked up would think I was a Yank, too. Hank nicknamed me D'Artagnan ("If it's good enough for the musketeers, kid, it's good enough for us"), and from then on we called ourselves the Four Caballeros. Hank also gave me a bunch of magazines—*Esquire, Look, Life, Saturday Evening Post*—which I carried around like medals of honor, and Gary taught me slang words that he said only GIs used. My metamorphosis was complete: I was now officially a Yank. I looked like a Yank, chewed gum like a Yank, even swaggered like a Yank. Trouble was, I didn't sound like a Yank. Try as they did, they couldn't teach me how to lose my London accent. That's when Buzz, who called every idea he had Good ol' American ingenuity, came up with "temporary laryngitis." This stroke of genius not only excused me from talking on dates, it brought me lots of sympathy as well—something my buddies, after seeing how well all the girls treated me, wished they'd thought of earlier for themselves. I mean, like Hank said: "Anything to get laid, right, kid?"

Not that finding sex was hard. Quite the opposite. "Like shooting fish in a barrel," was Gary's way of putting it. And he was right. Because at that time in the war, most young English girls were crazy about the Yanks. Buzz said it was because they were better cocksmen than the Limeys. I believed him at the time. But then, to be honest, I believed everything else he and the others said as well. But later, after the war, I realized it was more likely because the

Yanks had more money than British servicemen (and were happy to spend it); also they could give the girls what they couldn't get anywhere else, like, nylons, chewing gum, American cigarettes, and chocolate.

There was one drawback to this Utopian life I'd stumbled upon: because it was illegal for me, a Brit, to wear an American uniform I had to be careful where I wore it. London, especially the heart of London, was crawling with MPs—both British and American—and it seemed to me their one purpose in life was to check and recheck every serviceman's papers. Because of my age, Buzz said that even if I was picked up nothing much would happen to me. But, he warned, a lot could happen to them. And all of it bad. So I had to promise that if the MPs grabbed me, I would never say where I got the uniform from or that I even knew Buzz, Hank or Gary.

As it happened, a few weeks later all that became moot. May ended and all servicemen, Americans included, were confined to their bases. Then on June 6, the invasion of Normandy began.

I never saw Hank or Gary again. Both were killed on Omaha Beach. Buzz survived but was wounded and shipped back to the States. I learned this from a girl he'd dated while in London. She'd received a letter from him while he was recuperating in a military hospital. "He asked about you," Rita told me. "Said if I ever saw you I was to tell you not to give up on your dream."

It was the encouragement I needed. In 1949, shortly after turning seventeen, I ran off to Hollywood. There, I looked up Buzz. It took a while but I finally found him working in a garage-and-bodyshop near Vermont and Sunset. The neighborhood was rundown and depressing and not anywhere near Malibu. Nor was there a movie star in sight. We had coffee at a grimy little hotdog stand and talked for ten minutes and then I left. Buzz was not the man I remembered. He was bitter about losing his leg, smelled of stale beer and cigarettes and said he'd just gotten divorced. Then (and I don't know why he said this, unless he felt guilty or something) he said he'd lied to me in London; he'd never lived at Malibu and the only actors he knew were the has-beens he saw while collecting his unemployment check.

I don't know when I've ever been more disappointed. Which is why, after I left Buzz and took the big red street car to my room at the YMCA, I at first wished he'd been killed with Hank and Gary so that my memory of them would have always been as those young, happy, fun-loving Three Caballeros.

But then I got to thinking: If it hadn't been for their encouragement, I might never have been so determined to go to America. And that, when I think of how wonderful life here has been, would have been the biggest mistake I could have made.

✠

The Sins of the Father

*The evil that men do lives after them; the good is oft interred
with their bones*

– Shakespeare

Lower Trout Lake was a small, fish-shaped body of water about two hours drive south from Traverse City and within walking distance of the east shore of Lake Michigan. Fifty-two cottages ringed the lake, many of them half-hidden by the dense woods that grew right down to the water's edge. Most of the cottages were only occupied during the summer; the winters too cold and the snow too deep for all but the hardiest of folks to live there permanently.

Because the trout fishing was so good, and the lake so close to civilization, the cottages were at a premium and for the most part had been owned by the family for generations. When one did come up for sale, neighbors were immediately informed and usually the cottage was bought by friends-of-friends before a realtor ever had a chance to talk to the owners. That way, everything was kept in the family, so to speak. That's why it was such a shock to everyone on the lake when they heard that strangers had bought the Ben Hampton place. The residents were appalled. They couldn't blame Ol' Ben, because all he'd done was had the nerve to die suddenly from a stroke; but they could and did blame his son, Arnie, who owned a Chevy dealership in nearby Cherryton (a derivative of Cherry Town, so-named because the annual Cherry Festival was held there) and knew damn well that he should have notified the Trout Lake Committee about his intentions to sell the cottage. Of course, every member of the TLC knew why Arnie hadn't told them, because every one of them had voted not to let him join the committee so long as his dad was alive. Even so, they grumbled at their emergency meeting, Arnie didn't have to sink this low to get his revenge. One member suggested that they call Arnie and ask him to change his mind before the sale was final. It was a good idea except, typically, no one wanted to be the one who made the call. So the matter was tabled and everyone went home to wait and see just who these "strangers" were.

The people most interested, of course, were their next door neighbors, the Starbucks. Joe, the husband, was vice-president of the National Trust Bank in Traverse City. He remained in town all week and only joined his wife, Marianne, and son, Boone, on the weekends. Marianne and Boone, meanwhile, had moved into the lakeside cottage at the start of the summer vacation and planned to stay there until twelve-year-old Boone had to return to his school-for-special children.

"You're kidding me!" Joe said when his wife told him about the sale of the Hampton cottage. "Arnie sold it without telling anyone? Well, I'll be damned. I bet his old man's turning in his grave. What're they like, anyway? Have you met 'em?"

"No, but I've seen them. Mother and daughter, both."

"You don't sound too impressed."

"Well, I hate to say this, honey, because it sounds terribly prejudiced, but they look like trailer trash to me."

"Oh, great! I'll try to remember that next time Mr. Arnold Hampton wants to extend one of his loans."

⋅⊱ ⊰⋅

Boone Starbuck first met Havis Deighton the day after she and her mother moved in. He was sitting at the end of the narrow wooden dock fronting the cottage. It was his favorite spot in the whole world and every day he'd sit there for hours, contentedly staring out across the lake, doing nothing more than humming quietly to himself as he dangled his feet among the schools of silvery-blue minnows darting about in the shallow water.

This morning, he'd already been there for two hours when he felt a stranger walking up behind him. He knew it was a stranger because of the way the old flimsy dock shook. It didn't shake as much as when his mother or his father walked on it, so he knew it had to be someone smaller, lighter; someone he didn't know. He turned and saw a tall willowy girl of about fourteen approaching. She had long flame-red hair, odd yellow-green eyes and was pretty in an adult way. She wore a lot more makeup than his mother, and her lavender tank-top and frayed denim cutoffs fitted her like a second skin. She was hatless and barefoot and walked like her mom did, slinky-hipped and with her small firm breasts thrust out, like she was selling sex.

Boone didn't think she was sexy, because sex was something he didn't think about. But in his childlike mind he did wonder how she'd managed to squeeze into such tight clothes.

"Hi," she said, stopping beside him. "I'm Havis. Me'n Mom just moved in next door."

Boone stared blankly at her.

"What's your name?"

Boone, his mind still stuck on wondering how she could get in and out of her clothes, hesitated, then said vaguely: "Name?"

"Yeah, you know, like what other folks call you. Frank, Joey, Billy-Bob—what?"

Boone frowned, confused. He didn't know any of those boys.

"What's the matter? Don't you know your own name? Or don't you want to tell me? Which?"

"My name," he said slowly, "is… is… " He held up his left wrist so she could see the silver ID bracelet he wore.

Puzzled, Havis leaned close and saw his name, telephone number and blood type stamped on the plate. She studied Boone and shook her head in amazement.

"What d'you need that for? Can't you even re—?" About to say "remember your own name?" she broke off as she noticed his feet dangling in the water and saw he still had his shoes and socks on. She started to laugh, looked into his innocent blank-eyed face and stopped, suddenly realizing that something must be wrong with him. Her whole attitude softened. She said gently:

"Boone Starbuck. What a cool name. Okay if I sit next to you?" She sat before he could reply and smiled at him. "Know what, Boone? You'n me, we're gonna be friends."

Boone smiled, finally understanding something. "Good," he said. "Boone likes friends."

⸻

Earlier, when Havis had seen Boone sitting on the dock from her bedroom window, she'd thought at first he was just a lonely boy who had no friends, with nothing better to do than sit on a dock all day. But the more she watched him, the more she sensed this wasn't true: he was alone, yes, but he wasn't lonely. Quite the opposite. He was perfectly content. *He's like me,* she thought. He has no friends, but he's not lonely because he lives in his own little world. Intrigued that she'd found a soul-mate, Havis jumped off her bed and went outside to introduce herself.

Now, as she sat beside Boone at the end of the dock, she felt for the first time since her mother had said they were moving—*again*—as if she finally might have found a place where she could fit in. And if fitting in was too much to ask, then at the very least she and her mom might be able to live without being continually harassed by everyone around them. It was a lot to ask, she knew, when your father was a convicted serial killer sitting on death row in Texas, but, as her mother had said during their long drive north, "Baby girl, it don't cost nothin' to hope."

⤙⚫ ⚫⤚

After they'd sat there in silence for a few minutes, Havis' natural curiosity got the better of her.

"How come you didn't take your shoes'n socks off?"

"Shoes'n socks?"

"Yeah. What'd you do, forget you had 'em on?"

"No," Boone said. "Boone is a good boy. He never forgets to put his shoes'n socks on in the morning." He beamed, pleased with himself, and kicked his feet back and forth in the water.

"And your mom don't mind if you get 'em all wet?"

Boone wasn't listening; he was having too much fun kicking and splashing water everywhere.

"Hey, cool it! You're getting me soaked."

Boone laughed happily and kept on kicking. Irked, Havis grasped both his knees and tried to hold them down.

"Cut it out, okay? Or I won't be your friend."

A sadness almost beyond human understanding darkened Boone's face and he stopped kicking. He looked as if he were about to cry and immediately Havis wished she hadn't said anything.

"Oh, go ahead," she said. "Kick, if you want to. I can't get any wetter than I already am."

Boone didn't move. He sat as if frozen in time. Blue eyes wide open. Gaze fixed out across the gray, sun-whitened lake. Hands clasped in his lap. So still, it was impossible to tell if he was even breathing. Then, gradually, he started rocking. He rocked slowly at first and then faster, all the time humming; not the happy, sing-song, tuneless humming he'd been doing earlier but a strange, soft, high-pitched one-note humming that sound-ed like he was about to lose control; explode.

The humming grated on Havis' nerves and she told him to stop it. When he ignored her, she wagged a finger in his face and said: "You hear me? Stop it. I hate that weird sound."

Boone's high-pitched humming grew louder; more intense.

Havis lost her temper. "Fine!" she said, jumping up. "You want to keep making that sound, I'm outta here." She started to walk off, then stopped, confused, as she felt some strange mental connection pulling her back to Boone. She studied him and found herself thinking thoughts that not only weren't her own, but were so jumbled and childish she couldn't make sense of them. It felt like her mind had short-circuited. Wondering what was going on, Havis suddenly felt the dock shaking underfoot. She turned and saw a short, chunky blonde woman in a t-shirt and jeans, an apron around her waist, hands white with flour, hurrying toward her.

"It's okay," the woman said. "He'll calm down in a minute."

"I didn't do nothing to him," Havis said. "Honest."

"'Course you didn't," the woman said, reassuringly. She had the sweetest, friendliest face Havis had ever seen. "You don't have to do anything to set him off. He does that all by himself, poor lamb." She knelt behind Boone, put her arms around him and gently shushed him. "Shhhh, there's my good boy, shhhhh, mom's here now, shhhhh, calm down, shhhh, everything's going to be all right, shhhhhhh."

Gradually, Boone stopped rocking and stopped humming. And the moment he stopped, he began smiling again. "Havis," he said, pointing at her but talking to his mother. "We're friends."

"I'm glad," she said. "It's always nice to have friends." She helped Boone to his feet, keeping one arm around him as she turned and extended her free hand to Havis. "I'm Mrs. Starbuck. Boone's mom."

"Nice to meet you, ma'am."

"I've got some hot biscuits ready to come out of the oven. I'm sure Boone would love to have you come and eat with us."

After Boone's mother had taken his shoes and socks off and dried his feet, they all sat at the kitchen table and ate the hot, wafery, mouth-watering biscuits with lots of sweet melting butter and fresh homemade cherry jam. Mrs. Starbuck poured milk for Boone but didn't seem surprised or offended when Havis said she preferred coffee. The cottage, which was really a three-bedroom wood-and-stone cabin, smelled like a bakery and was decorated like a New England farmhouse. Green plants hung in the windows, vases of flowers sat on the tables and counters, knick-knacks adorned the shelves and watercolor paintings of horses, red barns and Boston in the 1800s hung on the oak-paneled walls.

Havis, raised in sun-baked trailer courts, motels and tacky one-bedroom apartments throughout Texas and Oklahoma, looked about her in envious wonderment. She'd seen places like this in *Home and Garden*-type magazines in doctor's offices where her mom had worked, but she'd always thought they were decorated that way to sell whatever product they were advertising. Mrs. Starbuck must have read her thoughts because she explained that this was her husband's way of compromising; of trying to make her feel at home even though she was stuck in the middle of nowhere, hundreds of miles from her birthplace, which was just outside Cambridge. Havis nodded as if she understood, though she had no idea where Cambridge was and could not have cared less.

But when Mrs. Starbuck politely asked her where she and her mother were from, Havis knew if she told the truth the honeymoon would be over, so with a noncommittal shrug, she lied and said:

"Seattle."

Mrs. Starbuck frowned, surprised. She'd detected a slight twang to Havis' voice, she said, and had thought Havis and her mom came from somewhere like Texas or Oklahoma. Havis did what her mom had taught her to do whenever she was caught in a lie, she smiled; then she said that Mrs. Starbuck wasn't altogether wrong as she and her mom had recently spent some time in Oklahoma when they'd visited her Aunt Edith, who lived outside Tulsa.

"Mom'n me, we pick up accents real easy," she added. "Guess that's why we sound like we come from there." She knew from experience that the conversation would sooner or later get around to her father, so she again did what her mom told her to do and beat Mrs. Starbuck to the punch by saying: "We used to visit her a lot. You know. When my dad was alive. Aunt Edith being his cousin and all. But now, since there's just mom'n me, we mostly just talk to her on the phone." She paused as Boone suddenly reached across the table and grasped one of her hands, saying:

"Still friends?"

"'Course," Havis said. She got up and moved behind him, hugged him and kissed him on the top of the head. "We're gonna be friends for always."

"Always," repeated Boone. He rocked back and forth and hummed happily to himself. "Always is good."

◦─▷ ◁─◦

In the days that followed, Boone and Havis spent more and more time together. They played Frisbee on the sandy beach fronting their cottages, went swimming and boating on the lake, and, when it occasionally rained, they sat indoors and watched cartoons on television together. Actually, it was Havis who did everything; Boone, who had trouble grasping even the simplest of tasks, did his best to join in; but except for watching TV, which fascinated him, he always ended up giggling and limply clapping his hands.

At first, Mrs. Starbuck was wary of Havis, wondering, as she told her husband on the phone, why such a sharp little cookie would want to waste her time with someone like Boone. But as the days passed, and she saw how kind and patient Havis was with Boone, and how happily he responded, she relaxed enough to let them hike unsupervised through the woods to Lake Michigan. But first she made sure Havis understood that Boone needed constant watching and must never be left to wander around on his own.

"You don't have to worry about that," Havis assured her. "Boone follows me around like a shadow, even when I don't tell him to." To prove her point, she got up from the couch and went outside. The screen-door had barely banged shut behind her before Boone was up and following her. His mother watched through the window, marveling as Boone trotted along behind Havis like he was on a leash. First, she led him down to the water's edge, next around the old aluminum rowboat that was beached near the dock, then back up the path to the porch. There, Havis sat down and Boone sat obediently beside her. Havis got up; Boone got up. Havis stood on one leg; Boone did the same. Havis turned and smiled through the screen-door at Mrs. Starbuck.

"See what I mean?"

Mrs. Starbuck nodded. "I'm impressed."

Havis wasn't finished. Grinning as if she and Boone shared a secret, she looked at him and concentrated. As if signaled, he put his fingers in his mouth and pulled his lips apart, poked his tongue out and bleated like a goat. Then he knelt down, begged like a dog and barked.

Mrs. Starbuck wasn't amused. "Please, don't do that," she told Havis. "He's not a dog to teach tricks to, you know."

Havis stopped smiling. Boone stopped smiling. And when Havis, without warning, turned and headed for her cottage, Boone immediately traipsed after her. Havis stopped, looked at Boone but didn't say anything. Then she continued on home.

Boone returned to the porch, sat on the steps and burst into tears. His mother went out to calm him. But none of her usual methods could make him stop crying. Finally, when Mrs. Starbuck was at her wits' end, Havis reappeared. She carried two sticks of red licorice. She gave one to Boone, who'd stopped crying the moment he'd seen her approaching, and the other to Mrs. Starbuck.

"Keep this one where he can see it," Havis told her. "That way, he'll always know I'm coming back." She left before Mrs. Starbuck could argue. This time Boone watched her go, chewing contentedly on his licorice stick, humming to himself as if he didn't have a care in the world.

Troubled, Mrs. Starbuck went indoors and called her husband. She explained everything to him, but he didn't get it and asked her what the problem was. The problem, she said, was that Havis seemed to have more control over Boone than she, his mother, did. And she found that very unsettling. Her husband, who was in the middle of some important bank business, said he thought she was overreacting but if it bothered her, then she should stop Boone and Havis from playing together so often. And if that wasn't enough, tell Havis to stop coming over altogether.

"You obviously haven't been listening to a word I've said," Mrs. Starbuck said, and banged down the receiver. She then called her mother in Cambridge, Massachusetts, and explained everything that had happened.

"Do you think I'm overreacting, momma?"

Her mother was too wise to immediately agree with her, or to quickly condemn Joe. Instead, she took the middle road, advising Marianne not say or do anything about this right away; but to wait, watch and listen, and over the next couple of weeks see for herself if she was indeed overreacting or not. After all, Boone, sweet and adorable as he was, was a very strange boy and it was almost impossible to predict what he was thinking or was going to do next. If Marianne acted too hastily, and somehow damaged or even severed the relationship Boone had with this Havis girl, who knows how it would affect him in the long run? Whereas if Marianne waited, he may suddenly tire of Havis all by himself, or Havis tire of him, and then she, Marianne, wouldn't have to do anything and Boone could never feel his mother was responsible. "Of course," her mother concluded, "this is merely my opinion, dear, and to be honest with you I'm not too familiar with the latest ways of handling children with Boone's problems."

"Who is?" Mrs. Starbuck said with a heavy sigh. "Certainly not me, and I've been around him more than anyone."

But she took her mother's advice and for the next two weeks did nothing to hamper or restrict Havis from playing with Boone. She did, however, watch them very carefully from a distance, all the while trying to decide if their relationship, which grew closer all the time, was good for her son or unhealthy.

She only made one mistake; that was on a Saturday morning when she and her husband were drinking coffee on the porch, and she tried to describe what was going on. "It's the most amazing thing, Joe. When they first met, they used to talk all the time. Then, gradually, it got less and less. Now, they barely say two words to each other. Yet the longer you watch them together, the more you realize that they don't have to. Each one seems to know what the other's thinking."

"Really?"

Mrs. Starbuck nodded. "Considering Boone's handicap, and how shy he's always been around strangers, it's really quite remarkable. I mean, someone who'd never met them would think they'd known each other all their lives."

"Maybe they got a little ESP going?"

"Don't laugh. It wouldn't surprise me a bit. I've been around Boone continuously since he was born and I swear I don't know half of what's going on in his mind. But Havis, she seems to know just by looking at him." Mrs. Starbuck sighed and shook her head. "I tell you, honey, it's the damnedest thing… and sometimes a little bit scary."

"What's Havis' mom think about all this?"

"I think she's fine with it."

"You think? Mean, she's never talked to you about her daughter spending so much time with Boone?"

"She's never talked to me about anything. Good grief, we've been neighbors now for over a month and I hardly know the woman. We've said good-morning a few times, and once she came over and borrowed some coffee from me—said her brother was staying with them for a few days, and she'd run out."

"She pay you back?"

"The next day. Left a whole pound on the porch with a thank you note. But other than that, and a casual 'hi' now and then as we wave from our porches—we hardly see each… "

"What?" Joe said as his wife suddenly stopped and frowned.

"I was just wondering."

"'Bout what?"

"Why she lied about the man being her brother. I mean, it's obvious he isn't. You've only got to see them together, kissing, fondling each other, holding hands as they walk around the lake. Good God, what does the woman think we are, blind or something?"

"So she's got her boyfriend staying there—what's the big deal, Marianne? This day and age, I'd be surprised if she didn't."

"I wasn't thinking about them. I was thinking about Havis. What effect it might have on *her.*"

Joe Starbuck laughed. He was a big, good-natured man of forty-three, with brown curly hair, warm brown eyes and a quick engaging smile that put all his customers—even the ones who came in to borrow money—instantly at ease.

"Having seen the way that kid dresses and slinks around," he said, "I think we already know the answer to that. Hell, she brings new meaning to the term 'flaunting it.'"

"Joe, you don't have to be vulgar."

"I'm not being vulgar. Just stating a fact." Still amused, he added: "Maybe our son isn't as slow as we think. Maybe he knows she's hot, too, and that's why he hangs around with—"

"Stop it! That's a terrible thing to say."

"Why? It would mean he's got more on his mind than just watching the waves on the lake."

I said, stop it. And I mean it. It's sad enough that our only son has the mind of a—a—"

Idiot, thought her husband, and immediately hated himself for thinking it.

"—a two-year-old, without your making fun of him." She got up and stalked into the cottage, leaving Joe Starbuck staring at his son, who was screaming with laughter as he and Havis stood in the shallows of the lake, splashing water over each other. *You poor little guy,* he thought sadly. *What a lousy deal we gave you. Locked up in that mindless little world you live in, hell's fire, what kind of life have you got to look forward to... ?*

⊷ ⊶

That morning the two of them walked, hand-in-hand, through the woods and up over the towering sand dunes and on along the beach that ran for miles along the wind-swept shores of Lake Michigan. Except for a black Labrador named Buck, who lived in a big yellow house back in the woods, they were alone. Buck ran in circles around them, barking, wagging his tail and bringing them sticks to throw.

"You stupid dog," Havis told it. "Why should we throw sticks for you when you never go get then?"

"Throw?" Boone said, holding up a piece of driftwood. Havis shook her head, *no.* "Throw?" he repeated, eyes pleading. She started to shake her head again, saw he was ready to cry and gave in. "Oh, all right. Go ahead, throw the dumb thing. But don't cry this time when he doesn't bring it back, okay?"

Boone giggled and threw the stick. It landed about thirty feet from the shore and floated on the incoming waves. Buck ran barking into the surf. But as soon as the water reached up to his chest, the lab stopped, whirled around and came running back to them. He stopped at their feet, shook water all over them, barked once, then ran up the dunes and vanished into the woods.

Boone started crying.

"I told you," Havis said. "Next time, maybe you'll listen to me."

Boone cried even harder. Havis put her arm around him and kissed the top of his head. "Poor baby," she said. "You just don't get it, do you?" She took his hand, "C'mon, let's run," and together they ran along the beach.

Presently, they rounded Bear Dunes and came within sight of the light-house. Built on top of a steep cliff called Point Dune, the lighthouse had long ago been closed down and now had a wire fence around the property with signs warning trespassers to keep out or be fined. Boone pointed to the tall, graceful white tower and looked eagerly at Havis. She looked into his bright empty eyes and, reading his mind, nodded. "Be fun, wouldn't it?" she said. "But we'd have to sneak in at night. Otherwise folks might see us and call the cops." She looked at her watch, saw it was getting late, and started back the way they'd come. Boone didn't want to stop looking at the lighthouse, but he also didn't want to lose Havis. The dilemma was too much for his muddled brain and he started to hum in a high-pitched voice.

Havis stopped and looked back at him. "Cut it out, you dork. You know I hate it when you make that sound."

Her sharp tone increased his agitation. His eyes darted about. He clenched and unclenched his fists. His high-pitched humming grew more intense.

Havis felt sorry for him. But a cruel uncontrollable urge overrode her tenderness and made her pick up a stick. Handing it to him, she stared into his eyes. He stared back at her as if hypnotized. His humming stopped. He sagged like a scolded child. Still she stared into his eyes. He wilted, distressed by what she was telling him to do. For another moment he tried to resist her silent command. But finally she won out and slowly he began whipping himself across the buttocks.

"Boone's a bad boy," he said in rhythm with his whipping. "Boone's a very, *very* bad boy."

Havis let Boone hit himself a dozen times, then stuck out her hand. He obediently handed her the stick.

Pleased with herself, Havis looked into his tearful eyes and concentrated. She willed herself to send Boone's hapless brain a message, thinking: *Next time you disobey me, you won't ever see me again. Remember that.*

Boone's last flimsy link to reality crumbled. Mind churning in chaos, he started sobbing. Part of Havis felt sorry for him. Another part didn't. They fought a moment. Then Havis couldn't control the sadistic urge that swept through her and she thought: *Eat sand, you little monster.*

Boone, still sobbing, dropped to his knees and began to eat handfuls of sand. It was a pathetic sight. Havis watched him, eyes slitted, lips drawn back in a cruel smile. Then, with her sadistic tendencies satiated, she broke free of whatever private demon she'd been captured by, and, as if seeing what Boone was doing for the first time, instantly regretted her actions. She knelt before him, her voice gentle as she told him to stop.

Boone just looked at her, mouth slackly open, sand drooling from his lips. Tenderly, Havis took her sleeve and wiped away the sand. "I'm *so* sorry," she told him. "I don't know why I did that. I'm not really a mean person, you know. I'd never hurt you intentionally. It just sort of, well, happened."

Boone wiped away his tears and stared at her like a scolded puppy asking to be forgiven.

"It'll never happen again. I promise." She took his hand, "C'mon, let's go home," and led him toward the woods.

That night as Mrs. Starbuck bathed Boone in the bathtub, she noticed the faint bruises that smudged his bottom. By now they had lost most of their redness, but were still visible on his white skin. She examined them, concerned, then asked him how he'd gotten them. Boone giggled. His mother patiently explained that it wasn't funny, and repeated her question. Boone looked blankly at her. Then he grabbed the rubber dinosaur floating in the bathwater and smacked it on the butt. *Bad Dino,* he told it. *Very bad Dino.*

Not making the connection, his mother gently took the toy dinosaur from him and placed it on the edge of the tub. Boone responded by angrily grabbing the dinosaur and beating it against the wall, shouting "Bad! Bad! Bad!" And when his mother tried to take it from him, he lost control and did something he'd never done before: threw it in her face. Then, humming wildly, he pounded his fists in the water, drenching his startled mother. Shocked by his unexpected violence, she did what the psychiatrist who treated Boone had told her to do if she ever felt he was out of control: she picked up the bath towel and covered herself. She then sat perfectly still on the floor.

It took a few minutes, but finally Boone calmed down and turned his attention to his mother. A strange, pathetic little whimper came from him. Then he climbed out of the bath, sat down beside his mother, lifted up one side of the towel and tried to cuddle up close to her. She waited until he was settled. Then, keeping the blanket over them, she put her arm about his still-wet bare shoulders and kissed his cheek. "My poor sweetie," she whispered to him. "If only I knew how to help you... make you feel better... "

⇥ ⇤

The next morning Mrs. Starbuck waited on the porch steps for Havis to come over and then confronted her about the bruises on Boone's bottom. Did she know how he'd gotten them? Havis said she didn't even know Boone *had* any welts on his bottom. Or any place else for that matter. He never took his clothes off in front of her, she added with just the right amount of modesty.

But if she had to guess, she said, he probably got them when he was sliding down the dunes yesterday. They'd found an old garbage bin lid, she explained, and pretended it was a sled and the sand was snow and spent the afternoon sliding down the slopes. Both of them kept falling off, but the sand was soft so she hadn't thought it mattered. "I'm sorry that he got hurt, Mrs. Starbuck. Next time I'll know better."

Marianne Starbuck seemed to accept her explanation without question and Havis considered the subject closed. But she'd learned a valuable lesson. Next time she punished Boone, she'd do it in a way that left no incriminating marks.

After the children left for their walk around the lake, Mrs. Starbuck went into the office adjoining the garage, turned on her computer and tried to figure out a way to find out some personal information about their new neighbors. She felt ashamed for doing it, and wondered what it was about Havis' explanation that she didn't believe. Whatever it was escaped her, so she put it down to a mother's intuition and began typing an email to Arnie Hampton. She was thinking of trading her Volvo in for a Chevy Blazer, she wrote, and would like to discuss what kind of a deal he'd give her. Please get back to her ASAP. Regards, Marianne. P.S., she added. Please don't say anything about this to Joe yet as he'll find nine million reasons why she should keep her Volvo.

That ought to get a response, she thought as she sent off the email. Knowing Mr. Arnold Hampton's greedy little mind the way she did, he'd probably offer to drive right over on the spot.

She wasn't far wrong. Arnie's return email appeared on her monitor within ten minutes. Be happy to, it said. And even as she was reading the message, the phone rang. She hit the speaker button, "Hello, Arnie," she said, laughing. "Busted," Arnie said. "Man, no weeds growing on Little Miss Marianne, is there?" He then told her that he was going to be in her area around noon and if she was free, why didn't she meet him for lunch. "That oughta start a few tongues a-waggin', right, princess?"

They met at the Cherry Hut, a small home-style restaurant famous for large portions and every kind of food that involved cherries, from pies to ice cream to salad dressing. Arnie was in his usual rush-rush mode, so immediately after they'd ordered he handed her a computer printout containing prices and statistics about Chevy Blazers and Blue Book trade-in values for Volvos.

Marianne Starbuck scanned the printout, then tucked it in her purse, saying she wanted to study it carefully in the peace and quiet of her home. As Arnie looked disappointed, she smiled her brightest smile and said there was another reason why she wanted to talk to him: could he give her some background info on the Deightons. Arnie looked blankly at her. Deightons? He didn't know any Deightons. Sure he did, Marianne said. He'd just sold his dad's cottage to them, remember? Their name wasn't Deighton, Arnie said. The woman who'd bought the cabin was Mrs. Crisler. Ruby Crisler, "You know, like the car only without an 'h' and with an 'I' instead of a 'y.'"

"You sure?"

"Absolutely." He leaned forward and lowered his voice to a conspiratorial whisper. "But it makes sense that she'd want to change their name. I would too if I was married to a convicted serial killer."

"Arnie—"

"I'm serious, princess. You must've heard about him. It was all over the TV. About seven or eight years ago. Killed six young boys and is now on death row in a Texas prison."

Marianne Starbuck was so shocked, she lost her voice.

"'Cause of him," Arnie went on, "his wife and kid had to keep moving from town to town. Nobody wanted them in their neighborhood. Kept harassing them until they moved away. Took 'em all this time but finally they worked their way up to this neck of the woods."

"And you found this out when?" Marianne gasped. "Before or after you sold them the cottage?"

"After." Arnie made a face. "But the way I feel about those bastards on the TLC, I'd've sold it even if I'd known. You and Joe don't have to worry," he said, seeing her look. "It was Harley Crisler who done the murdering, not his wife and kid."

Suddenly, Marianne wasn't hungry. "One last thing," she said. "It's probably not important, but I have to be sure."

"Shoot."

"The daughter, Havis... the mother didn't happen to mention if she'd ever been in any kind of trouble, did she?"

"Nah," Arnie said. "It's like I told you—"

"I know," Marianne finished for him, "Harley's the one who did the murdering. Well, let me tell *you* something, Mr. Arnold Hampton. Joe and you grew up together and your fathers were best friends. Don't you think you owed it to us to at least *mention* this little horror story?" When he didn't answer, she added angrily: "And by the way, Arnie. I don't believe that you didn't know their real name. You had to know it before you finalized the sale, otherwise, when you transferred the deed, it wouldn't have been legal." Rising, she slammed several loose bills down on the table and stormed out.

⇥ ⇤

Fear, not the hot weather, made Marianne Starbuck break into a sweat as she drove home. She wasn't sure what caused the fear; as a rational woman, common sense told her that just because Harley Crisler had murdered six young boys didn't mean that Havis would murder Boone. Nothing she'd ever read proved or even suggested that killers passed their murdering instincts on to their children. And yet, hard as she tried to convince herself that she was being foolish and over-reacting, a tiny nagging voice in the back of her mind kept warning her that she wasn't; that Boone's life was in immediate jeopardy.

When she reached the cottage, Marianne found Havis and Boone in the kitchen. A saucepan lay in a puddle of water on the floor and Havis was rubbing butter onto the blistered palm and fingers of Boone's right hand. He wasn't crying now but his eyes were watery and his cheeks tear-stained, and when he saw his mother he held up his burned hand and said: "Boone bad. Burn himself."

"It was my fault," Havis put in. "I was making us hotdogs for lunch—you know, like you said we could—and as I was taking the buns out of the toaster oven, I didn't see him grab the handle of the saucepan."

"Let me see that," Marianne said. She gently took Boone's hand from Havis and looked at the raw, badly blistered skin.

"Boone bad," he said.

"No you're not," Havis told him. "It was an accident. And anyway, if anyone's bad, it's me for letting you hurt yourself. If I hadn't turned my back on you—"

"Dammit, that's enough!" Marianne yelled. She felt herself losing control. It was uncharacteristic of her. And as both children turned to her, surprised by her outburst, she heard herself say: "I think Dr. Heiden should look at this. It's a really nasty burn and I don't want Boone to be scarred."

Havis nodded, agreeing. Her yellow-green eyes narrowed as she locked gazes with Marianne. "Want me to go with you?"

It was the last thing Mrs. Starbuck wanted. She shook her head, Havis' intense baleful gaze making her uneasy. "No, that's okay," and then to Boone, "Momma's going to take you for a nice ride. Won't that be fun?"

It wasn't until she was driving away, with Boone securely buckled-in in back, that Marianne realized she hadn't even asked Havis if she'd been burned.

⊸⊸▣ ▣⊶⊶

After Mrs. Starbuck and Boone had driven off, Havis wandered down to the water's edge. There, shading her eyes from the glaring sun, she watched a speedboat pulling a bikini-clad water-skier across the middle of the lake. A sunburned teenage boy steered the boat with one hand and waved to the girl with the other. Their laughter, mingled with the roar of the speedboat, echoed tauntingly in Havis' ears. A wave of bitter hatred aimed at both of them swept through her. What right did they have to be happy when she couldn't be? She hadn't asked to be born, any more than they had, so why was life slanted so unfairly against her and so obviously in favor of *them?* As usual, there was no answer. Life sucked, as her mom's boyfriend was always saying, and that's all there was to it. Oh yeah, thought Havis. No way! She wasn't going to stand meekly by as life steam-rollered her. She was going to fight back, to find a way to be one of the people enjoying life *in* the speedboat, not *on* the shore watching it!

Out on the lake the skier suddenly fell, her body tumbling over in the frothy wake. The speedboat made a long lazy turn and headed back to pick her up. A voice in Havis' head wished the boat would explode or that the propeller would cut off the girl's legs. Then another voice, weaker than the first, scolded her for thinking such hateful thoughts. *Things could be worse, always remember that,* the voice warned. Your mom may be trailer trash; and considering the number of beer-guzzling boyfriends she's brought home during the last few years, she might even be the whore everyone calls her; but at least she wasn't a drunk, like some mothers Havis knew; and she didn't beat up on her daughter, either. And if she wasn't home as much as Havis would've liked, well, it wasn't only because she was hanging out in bars but also because she was busting her butt working in some dumb doctor's office or as a waitress in some creepy diner where truckers kept hitting on her. And remember, the voice concluded, any money her mom made, she gladly shared with her daughter—

"Havis!"

Her thoughts interrupted, Havis looked back at their cottage and saw her mother waving to her from the front porch. "Honey, Jeff'n me are gonna take a little nap, okay?"

Havis, knowing what that meant, waved to show she understood and watched her mother return indoors. As the screen-door banged shut behind her, Havis felt as if it had cut her off from the last vestige of hope she'd ever had of being loved; of belonging anywhere; and immediately she felt an intense wave of loneliness smothering her. With the loneliness came an equally intense desire to be inside the cottage; a desire that an instant before the door closed, had been the farthest thought from her mind.

Answering that desire, she left the beach and made her way around to the back of the cottage. Her mother's bedroom window was open and Havis could hear the all-too-familiar grunts and groans of her mom and Jeff having sex. Often in the past, she'd watched them through a crack in the door of whatever apartment or motel they were staying in; today, she had no interest in what they were doing. She crept around the side of the cottage to her own bedroom window, quietly climbed inside and curled up among all the stuffed animals piled on her bed. As always, their fuzzy warmth comforted her. But as she cuddled her favorite, a large floppy-legged giraffe, she was surprised to feel it had a wet face. It was only then that Havis realized she was crying.

⇒▷◁◁　　◁◁▷⇐

She didn't remember falling asleep. But the next thing she heard was voices. She opened her eyes and realized it was dark. She got up and opened her door a crack. At the end of the hallway she saw her mother, in a pink satiny robe and with her back to Havis, standing at the front door talking to Mrs. Starbuck. She couldn't hear everything they said, but understood enough to know that Boone's mother was making it clear that she didn't want Havis playing with him anymore. When Havis' mom asked why not, Mrs. Starbuck replied that it didn't have anything to do with Havis, who was a fine young girl, but because Boone was becoming unruly without adult supervision; and that her son's analyst had advised her to be with him around the clock for the next few weeks or else she might lose control of him forever.

Havis quietly shut the door and sat on her bed, staring out the window at the sickle moon hanging above the treetops. *Serves you right,* she told herself. *If you hadn't told Boone to touch the handle of that hot saucepan just for*

*the fun of hearing him scream, he wouldn't have burned himself and you'd still
have him for a friend. As it stands now, you're back to where you were when
you got here: alone.*

She hated herself very much at that moment. She also hated her father,
even more than usual, for being who he was. Because she was sure now that
the uncontrollable sadistic urges she got came directly from him. All the years
of teasing at school she'd endured, all the ugly gossip she'd overheard, all the
whispered comments suggesting that she might possess some of her father's
traits—all these accusations weren't just "a bunch of ignorant bastards pissin'
in the wind," as her mother always claimed, but were in fact the truth: she
was her father's daughter; and since her father was a vicious sociopath who
got his kicks raping and murdering young boys, her future didn't look too
promising.

A voice inside her head said: *We'll show them. If everyone thinks you're
so bad, why not do something to prove them right?*

It was after midnight and the sky was black with rainclouds. In the Starbuck cottage the old grandfather clock sonorously chimed its final twelfth
stroke and then fell silent. Marianne Starbuck yawned, turned off the TV and
got up from the couch where she'd been watching the weather report. A cold
front had moved down from Canada, bringing high winds and the threat of
thunder-storms. Marianne made sure the porch shutters were secure and the
back and front screen-doors were latched, then headed for her bedroom. On
the way, she poked her head into Boone's room. By the glow of the tiny night-
light plugged in by his bed, she saw he was asleep on his side, his bandaged
hand showing whitely above the covers. She sighed, relieved. Earlier she'd
reluctantly given him a pain pill to deaden the throbbing of his burned hand.
As usual, he hadn't wanted to take it—since birth he'd had an aversion to taking any kind of pill—but she'd insisted, knowing that without it he wouldn't
get any sleep. As a result, he'd grown very agitated and difficult to handle and
it had taken all of her patience not to lose her temper with him. But finally
she'd gotten him calmed down and together they'd watched TV, shared a box
of chocolate chip cookies and hot milk and then she'd read him a bedtime
story and put him to bed.

Now, as she watched him sleeping, she reassured herself yet again that
she and Joe had made the right decision in not putting Boone in a home
for special children, as some of the therapists they'd been counseled by had
recommended. Raising a baby like Boone was extremely difficult, they'd
explained; so difficult, it often caused marital problems and even divorces.
Before Marianne and Joe committed themselves to this lifelong task—and

it *would* be lifelong, because Boone would almost certainly never mature beyond four or five years old—perhaps they needed to discuss it some more. No, Marianne said before Joe could speak, she and her husband had already discussed it thoroughly and both agreed that since she couldn't have any more children, they wanted their son with them, not growing up with strangers in a hospital or home for special children. Isn't that right, honey? she added to Joe. After a slight hesitation, he nodded and put his arm around her to show the doctors that he supported her all the way. But she'd noticed his hesitation and later, when they were driving home, she burst into tears and accused him of not wanting their child. Already feeling guilty for the way he felt, Joe pulled over to the side of the road and for the next half-hour said everything he could to convince her that she was wrong. Marianne finally said she believed him, though deep down she didn't, and they drove home and made love even though her heart wasn't in it.

After that, on the surface at least, everything seemed to be the same between them. But both knew it wasn't; knew it would never be the same. Joe would never have the son he wanted, the son to mold into his own image, and though Marianne knew he tried his best to enjoy Boone, she could tell he resented the boy and felt that God had cheated him out of his rightful heir. It was a painful realization, but Marianne saw it happening right before her eyes. Being around Boone increased Joe's resentment, and to shield himself from the pain he began burying himself more and more in his work. He then found reasons to stay in Traverse City rather than make the two-hour drive home, and finally rented an apartment there and only came home on the weekends.

And all because of you, Marianne thought as she gazed at her peacefully sleeping child. *Well, I don't care. To me, you're worth it; you're worth anything. And though I'll never be able to make you understand that, or how much I really love you, at least I'll always be here to look after you and make your life as pleasant as possible.*

⇒▣◉ ◎▣⇐

From where she crouched in the bushes outside Boone's bedroom, Havis could just see over the edge of the window-frame. It was dark and she was sure no one could see her. Overhead, ghostly black clouds covered the moon and Havis felt the wind tugging at her hair. She peered through the screen-covered window. There was a gap between the louvered blinds and through it she watched as Boone's mother, silhouetted against the light in the hall, closed his bedroom door. Havis guessed that she'd gone to bed. To make sure she wasn't coming back, Havis waited ten minutes or so before straightening up and quietly tapping on the screen. Boone stirred restlessly, but didn't waken. She tapped again, louder. This time he heard her and opened his eyes. She tapped again. He sat up and looked around, wondering where the tapping was coming from. Havis tapped once more on the screen and as Boone pushed aside the blinds, she held up the sketch she'd drawn of the lighthouse. Boone blinked, as if not believing what he saw; then, as he realized it was Havis, he beamed and waved at her. She put a finger to her lips, silencing him, and motioned for him not to move. She then took out a screwdriver, pried open the screen, slid up the lower half of the window and quietly climbed inside. When he was dressed, she helped him put on some rubber boots and a yellow slicker she'd found in the closet, then helped him climb out of the window. Boone wasn't coordinated and Havis had a hard time getting him out without making a lot of noise. Finally, though, they were both outside. Havis waited a few seconds to see if they'd awakened Mrs. Starbuck. But when the only sound she heard was the wind rustling in the treetops, she took Boone's hand, turned on her flashlight and led him along the dirt trail that ran through the trees and ended at the dunes. The darkness of the surrounding woods and the eerie whining of the wind frightened Boone and he hung back, whimpering.

"Don't be a baby," Havis told him. "Don't you want to see the lighthouse?"

Boone shook his head, "'Fraid! 'Fraid!" he cried. He rolled his eyes and fearfully waggled his hands. "Boone go home now."

Growing impatient, Havis shook him and warned him to be quiet or she'd make him hurt himself. He only became more agitated.

Havis held the flashlight upward so both their faces were illuminated and stared into Boone's panic-filled eyes. She concentrated and willed him to be quiet. When he didn't respond, she concentrated harder. Nothing happened for a few moments; then Havis' brain waves recoiled as she was suddenly immersed in the churning turmoil of Boone's mind. It was like being jolted by an electric shock. She wanted to shut it off but knew if she did, she'd lose him. With great effort, she channeled all her thoughts into a single command and willed him to calm down.

Boone, as Havis' mind took control of his, grew quiet. The panic left his eyes; his expression became blank. *That's better,* her mind told him. *Now, follow me.* She continued on along the trail, Boone traipsing obediently beside her.

Thunder startled Marianne Starbuck out of a sound sleep. She lay there a moment, trying to collect herself, while outside a vivid flash of lightning showed through the louvered blinds, lighting up her bedroom. A second clap of thunder brought her leaping out of bed. Throwing on her robe, she ran out of the room and along the hallway to Boone's bedroom. He was terrified of thunder and lightning, and she wanted to comfort him before he became too hysterical to manage.

She stopped one step into his room, shocked by the sight of his empty bed and the blinds flap-flapping against the still-open window. "Oh-my-God—!" She ran to the bed, barely feeling the wind-blown piece of paper that wrapped itself around one bare ankle. But as she knelt on the bed to look out the window, she felt the paper and pulled it loose. She hadn't intended to look at it, but before she could toss it away the sketch on it caught her eye: Point Dune Lighthouse.

In the panic of the moment, the significance of the drawing didn't register, and Marianne threw it aside. She leaned out the open window, wind whipping her hair about her face, and shouted Boone's name several times. When he didn't answer, her panic increased. She pulled her head back inside and started for the door, intending to call the police. Then it dawned on her that Boone would never have crawled out of the window on his own— someone must have helped him; and the only person she knew who'd do that was—Havis!

Simultaneously, she remembered how well Havis could draw. Marianne grabbed up the piece of paper again and looked at the lighthouse. It was definitely not Boone's work; he could barely scrawl his name. But why, she wondered, would Havis bother to draw a lighthouse for Boone? He didn't care about lighthouses. He wanted people to draw him dogs and horses and—

Then it hit her. Havis was showing him where she was taking him.

She ran into the living room and called her husband. When he came on the line, voice leaden with sleep, she said: "Joe, wake up! I can't explain now. There isn't time. But Havis has taken Boone to Point Dune Lighthouse. I don't know why but it can't be for a good reason. Call the sheriff. Tell him to meet me at the lighthouse. I'm leaving now!" She hung up before he could argue or question her, threw on her raincoat and bolted out to her car.

→)===◉ ◉===(←

As Havis and Boone toiled up the steep sandy path leading to the top of the cliff, thunder rumbled overhead. Lightning followed, and suddenly it was raining. Boone whimpered and clung to Havis' arm. "It's okay," she told him. "It's only thunder. Havis'll look after you."

When they reached the cliff-top, the wind howling in off Lake Michigan pushed against them and whipped their faces with the rain. Havis kept Boone ahead of her so she could see him. He walked like a penguin, arms at his sides, body leaned forward, the rain running off the brim of his rain-hat onto his glistening yellow slicker. Havis paused, pulled the hood of her windbreaker over her head and secured it with the drawstring. Boone, once she let go of his hand, wandered off. Havis caught up with him and grabbed his arm, "No, this way, dummy!" leading him to the gate in the chain-link fence that surrounded the property. A rusty piece of wire kept the gate shut. Havis untwisted it and kicked the gate open. She pushed Boone ahead of her and followed him up the path to the deserted lighthouse. It towered above them, much bigger than it looked from the beach below, the top barely visible in the rain-soaked darkness. Havis led Boone to the door. It was padlocked. She picked up a rock, hammered open the padlock, and dragged Boone inside.

They stood, motionless, in the small, eerily-silent rotunda until their eyes grew accustomed to the gloom. Then Havis pushed Boone to the foot of the narrow iron staircase that spiraled up through two platforms and beyond, all the way to the upper galley that contained the light. With Boone reluctantly leading the way and Havis giving him an occasional push from behind, they started up the staircase. Their footsteps clanked hollowly on the iron steps, the noise echoing about them. Outside, thunder boomed and lightning lit up the sky. Boone whimpered and cringed with every clap of thunder, every flash of lightning; especially when they got close to the top and he could see the lightning through the windows encircling the light galley.

When they were almost to the top, something came rushing out of the darkness and flew, wings pounding, right past their faces. It was a bird, vanishing too fast into the darkness for them to know what kind, but startling enough to terrify Boone and make Havis gasp. Screaming, Boone whirled around and tried to push past Havis. She yelled at him to stop and shoved him away. When he came at her again, she lashed out at him with her flashlight, knocking him back onto the stairs. He sat there sobbing, face buried in his hands. She tried to will him to get up but her heart was still pounding and she couldn't concentrate. So she shone the light over him and said if he didn't get up and keep climbing, she'd leave him there forever. To emphasize her point, she started down the stairs. Boone lifted his face from his hands and wailed like a baby. Havis felt his pain in her mind and climbed back up beside him. He meekly gave her his hand. Squeezing past him, she led him up the final steps to the light galley.

The lenses and refracting prisms had been removed years ago; but the revolving metal platform that once held the light mechanism was still there, rusted and covered with cobwebs.

"There," Havis said above the noise of the storm, "we're here. At the very top. Now, aren't you glad you came?"

Boone giggled foolishly. But he wouldn't let go of her hand and rather than upset him again, she led him to the windows and together they looked at the storm raging outside. At least, Havis looked; Boone turned his head away, whimpering with fear.

"I love storms," she said, watching the rain lashing against the glass. "I know most people hate 'em, but I think they're awesome. 'Specially when it thunders. Then I feel like, you know, God's trying to talk to me."

Or the devil, she thought.

Marianne Starbuck drove recklessly fast along the winding highway that ran parallel to the woods hiding Lake Michigan. The storm had worsened since she'd left the cottage. Thunder and lightning threatened to rip open the sky. The wind hurled small branches and leaves at the speeding Volvo. The rain pounded so hard on the windshield, the wipers had to struggle to keep the glass clear. But Marianne barely noticed; she was too busy begging God not to let any harm come to her son.

After a mile or so, she turned off the highway onto a foot trail that entered the woods. Her headlights flared over a sign that warned NO VEHICLES BEYOND THIS POINT. Marianne ignored it and followed the trail as it snaked between the trees. The Volvo bumped over ruts and fallen branches, bouncing Marianne around. She clung to the wheel, one foot gunning the engine, the other jamming on the brakes to avoid sliding off the trail at every abrupt turn. And all the time praying, *Please dear God, don't let her hurt him, don't let her hurt him. Please. Please…*

Soon the trees thinned out and the trail ended at a vista point overlooking Lake Michigan. Marianne skidded to a stop, grabbed a flashlight from the glove compartment, jumped out and ran up the path leading to the lighthouse. At the top she paused by the fence and, buffeted by the wind, eyes squinted against the driving rain, looked around for Boone and Havis. When she didn't see them, the mother in her hoped for one instant that maybe, just maybe she was wrong about Havis bringing Boone here. Then, through the slanting rain, she saw the open gate swinging back and forth in the wind and all hope vanished. With a tiny sob, she pushed in through the gate and ran to the lighthouse.

High up in the light galley, Havis led Boone down two steps to the lower level and opened the door leading out to the narrow walkway that ran around the top of the lighthouse. Instantly, they were blasted by the wind and rain. Terrified, Boone jumped back. He'd been holding Havis' hand and his sudden movement spun her around, causing her to drop her flashlight. It landed on the metal floor and rolled toward the spiral stairway. Havis tried to grab it, but she was too late: the flashlight rolled off the edge and bounced clanking down the stairs. Momentarily, Havis followed its path by the flashing beam; then the bulb broke and everything went dark.

"Satisfied?" she said angrily to Boone. "Now we can't see a thing!" As if to prove her wrong, a flash of lightning lit up the galley and showed the terror in Boone's eyes. He whimpered and spittle drooled from his mouth. When she didn't respond he shuffled toward her, searching for tenderness. Instead, his fear ignited Havis' mean streak. "You think you're scared now," she said, grabbing his arm, "wait till you're outside. You'll really piss your pants." She pushed him out the door onto the walkway. Boone stumbled, almost falling as the wind hit him, then kept himself upright by grabbing the guardrail. Havis shut the door and bolted it, then watched him through the rain-streaked window.

Outside, Boone clung desperately to the guardrail, sensing more than knowing that if he let go he'd be blown off onto the rocks below. The wind ripped his hat off. Boone moaned as it flew away. He looked back, squinting to see through the rain, and saw Havis' face pressed against the window. He cried out to her. She waved mockingly to him. Bewildered, he let go of the railing and in one lurching step, fell against the window. He pawed helplessly at the glass, imploring her to let him in.

"What?" Havis said, cupping a hand to her ear. "What'd you say?" Then: "Sorry, dummy, I can't hear you."

As Boone went on pawing and blubbering, Havis heard someone coming up the spiral stairway. She looked down and saw the beam of a flashlight climbing toward her; behind the beam came Boone's mother.

"Go back," Havis screamed at her. "Don't come up here!"

"Where's Boone?" Marianne demanded. "What've you done with him?"

"I'm warning you, Mrs. Starbuck. You come any farther and I'll kill him."

Marianne stopped, heart hammering in her chest, and shone the flashlight onto Havis' face.

"No… please, don't hurt him."

"Then, go back."

Marianne continued to hold the flashlight beam on Havis' face. "Why're you doing this? What'd Boone ever do to you?"

"Nothing. But he's dumb and stupid and he wants to die."

"No, he doesn't," said Marianne. "Poor baby's not bright enough to know *what* he wants."

"Then, why'd he tell me he did?"

"I don't believe you. How could he tell you something like that when he can barely string two words together?"

"He don't have to talk. I can read his mind. Bet you didn't know that, did you? Well, I can. I can make him do things too, anything I want, and if you come up here I'm gonna make him jump off—" She paused as behind

Marianne, far below, the beam of a powerful flashlight lit up the darkness and a man's voice called out:

"Mrs. Starbuck, you up there?"

Keeping the light shining in Havis' face, Marianne shouted, "Yes, sheriff. We're all up here." Then, to Havis: "Please, let me come up. I'm not going to hurt you. I just want my son."

Havis screamed, "No!" and ran to the door. Unlocking it, she stepped outside and joined Boone on the walkway.

Marianne shouted, "Hurry, sheriff, she's going to kill him," and scrambled up the stairway as fast as she could.

When she reached the lower level of the light galley, she paused and through the window saw Boone and Havis on the walkway. Both clung to the guardrail, backs to the wind. Marianne jerked open the door and stepped outside. Rain slashed against her face and a gust of wind almost lifted her off her feet. She dropped the flashlight, gripped the doorway with both hands and begged Havis to bring Boone inside.

Havis shook her head and grabbed Boone's arm. "Go away," she shouted, "or I'll push him over."

"No, don't! Please don't," Marianne begged her. "Let him go. He's all I've got. Please," she repeated when Havis didn't answer. "I'm begging you. Let him go."

Havis still didn't answer; didn't move.

"You don't want to kill him," Marianne told her. "Boone loves you… trusts you… knows you'd never hurt him."

Behind Marianne Sheriff Huddensack loomed in the doorway.

"Let the boy go," he said, shining his light in Havis' face. "You hear me, missy? I said… let-him-go."

Havis ignored him. For a long, agonizing moment she stared at Marianne. In her mind, two demons were fighting each other for total control and one was losing. Before the outcome was final, Havis suddenly jerked Boone's hands from the guardrail. And, even as Marianne screamed *no,* Havis pushed Boone toward her.

Mother and son stumbled into each other's arms. As they stood there hugging, battered by the wind and rain, the sheriff grabbed them from behind and pulled them into the lighthouse.

Overhead, thunder boomed and lightning lit up the sky.

Havis looked up, her rain-streaked face illuminated by the lightning, and shouted to the heavens:

"See, I'm not my father!"

Then she turned, saw the sheriff coming toward her and threw herself over the guardrail.

✠

www.ingramcontent.com/pod-product-compliance
Lightning Source LLC
Chambersburg PA
CBHW051146020726
47501CB00005B/1696